Mary Louise Booth, Jean Macé

Macé's Fairy Book

Home Fairy Tales

Mary Louise Booth, Jean Macé

Macé's Fairy Book
Home Fairy Tales

ISBN/EAN: 9783337081591

Printed in Europe, USA, Canada, Australia, Japan

Cover: Foto ©Andreas Hilbeck / pixelio.de

More available books at **www.hansebooks.com**

MACÉ'S FAIRY BOOK.

HOME FAIRY TALES

(CONTES DU PETIT-CHÂTEAU).

By JEAN MACÉ,

Editor of the *Magasin d'Éducation*; Author of "The Story of a Mouthful of Bread," etc., etc.

TRANSLATED BY MARY L. BOOTH,

Translator of "Martin's History of France," "Laboulaye's Fairy Book," etc., etc.

With Engravings.

NEW YORK:

HARPER & BROTHERS, PUBLISHERS,

FRANKLIN SQUARE.

By JEAN MACÉ.

HOME FAIRY TALES (*Contes du Petit-Château*). Translated by MARY L. BOOTH. With Engravings. 12mo, Cloth, $1 75.

THE SERVANTS OF THE STOMACH. Reprinted from the London Translation, Revised and Corrected. 12mo, Cloth, $1 75.

THE HISTORY OF A MOUTHFUL OF BREAD: and its Effect on the Organization of Men and Animals. Translated from the Eighth French Edition by Mrs. ALFRED GATTY. 12mo, Cloth, $1 75.

THE HISTORY OF THE SENSES AND THOUGHT. Translated by MARY L. BOOTH. 12mo. (*In Press.*)

PUBLISHED BY HARPER & BROTHERS, NEW YORK.

FROM THE AUTHOR TO THE TRANSLATOR.

DEAR MISS BOOTH,—

Receive my thanks for the honor which you have done my tales in translating them for your *young American friends*, as you write me.

Should they also become mine on reading you, you will have procured me in your country the only serious recompense to which a writer can aspire.

Good thoughts have the happy privilege of being every where at home, and souls have a common country in the human conscience. What I have attempted for my part to give to the children of my country, I am too happy that you should have judged worthy of being presented to the children of America. May it, in entering their souls, develop there those sentiments of honor, justice, and goodness which we are all commissioned to diffuse around us, and compared with which the ocean is but a brook!   JEAN MACÉ,

Professor in the School of the Little Castle.

Beblenheim, April 9, 1867.

A

TRANSLATOR'S PREFACE.

WE owe our first acquaintance with the unique and interesting collection of fairy tales now presented to American readers to the kindness of M. Edouard Laboulaye, who commended it to our attention some time since as one of the most successful books of the kind published in France. The perusal thereof will soon justify the popular verdict. The fairies here are good fairies—home fairies—each of whom has a mission to correct some childish fault, but who does her work so attractively and unobtrusively that the children for whom it is designed never think of rebelling against the moral which it is sought to convey. The stories are singularly pleasing and original, and older readers than the audience for whom they are written can not fail to be charmed with their ingenuity.

It may not be inappropriate to say in this connection a few words concerning the author, who, though one of the most popular writers for children in France, is as yet comparatively but little known in this country; and also to explain the origin of the, at first sight, incomprehensible title of the book, Tales of the Little Castle, to which, with the author's consent, we have prefixed that of Home Fairy Tales, as expressive of the spirit of the work.

Jean Macé was born in Paris, April 22, 1815. He was educated at the college Stanislas, where he subsequently filled the post of Professor of History, also performing divers professional duties in the colleges of Louis le Grand and Henri IV. He then entered the army, where he served for three years, after which he became the secretary of the celebrated Theodore Burette, his former Professor of History, with whom he remained until the death of this distinguished man in 1847. In the interval he contributed to various journals, and grew deeply interested in the political agitation which pervaded France during the crisis that supervened. In 1848 he assumed the editorship of the journal *La République*, which he continued to conduct until the *coup d'état* of 1851 blasted his hopes, and forced him to exile himself from the capital. He took refuge with his friend Mademoiselle Verenet, the principal of a young ladies' boarding-school at Beblenheim, a little village romantically situated in Rhenish France, under the shadow of the Vosges, between Strasbourg and Basle, not far from Colmar. In this lovely spot, some thirty years ago, Mademoiselle Verenet, then an invalid seeking health from the bracing air of the mountains, had built a tasteful châlet among the vines, which the villagers admiringly christened the Little Castle. To amuse her loneliness, a little cousin was sent her to bring up, then another, and then a third; her health improved with her multiplied cares; the number of her charges meanwhile increased, and the house grew in proportion to its inmates, until finally the authorities bestirred themselves, and demanded that the mistress of this improvised school should obtain the sanction of the government to her enterprise. It would have been too hard to scatter the loving circle that had clustered together. Mademoiselle Verenet complied with the necessary requirements, and her home-school became a recognized educational institution. We will leave M. Macé to tell the story of his introduction thereto in his own words:

"This was in 1850. I was at that time given up to the political fever which took possession of so many minds after the Revolution of 1848. I was traveling in the east of France, for the purpose of organizing the correspondence of a journal. Having been charged by one of Mademoiselle Verenet's pupils with a commission for her daughter, I knocked one day at the gate of the Little Castle, and, I must confess, my heart beat somewhat; to a shy man like me, a young ladies' school was something very imposing. I met on my way a lady, simply dressed, standing on a mound; it was the mistress of the house, who was superintending the erection of an asylum which she was building for the children of the village. I little suspected at that moment that the asylum was before me which would one day shelter my life. My coming had been announced. Introduced without ceremony among the pupils, I was quite surprised to feel myself at ease. I had expected something stiff and tiresome. I was in a large country house, inhabited by a family more numerous than usual; that was all. I was invited to make some remarks; I learned afterward that I was successful. Emboldened by the atmosphere of universal kindness that surrounded me, I even collected the memories of my old vocation of professor, and ventured to interfere in a lesson of natural philosophy wherein the teacher had met with some difficulty, which was not strange, with the book that she held. It appears that I had the good fortune to make myself understood.

"This day, passed free from the angry disputes and colloquies with government officials which had occupied my life for the past five months, and which I would encounter again on the morrow, was to me like a halt in a cool oasis, and I carried away a remembrance of the house, which was kept up by correspondence.

"When the gust of December, 1851, came, I was among the leaves that it swept away; but, happier than many others, I flew to the little paradise, the image of which had remained present to my mind. I was invited to fill the post of Professor of the Natural Sciences ; but, ere long, attracting to myself all branches of instruction, from book-keeping to geology, together with history and literature, I abandoned myself with daily increasing delight to the happiness of intellectual and moral paternity, the chief of the social functions when the soul is raised to a level with its vocation. I was at last in my true calling. After capriciously trying a little of every thing, it was found that I was born for a professor in a young ladies' school."

In this quiet retreat M. Macé remained buried with his family for ten years. He first gave signs of life by the publication, in 1861, of the story of a Mouthful of Bread, or Letters to a Child on the Digestive Organs, a juvenile physiological work which achieved great success. This was afterward followed by Tales of the Little Castle, the Theatre of the Little Castle, Grandpapa's Arithmetic, A Journey to the Country of Grammar, the Servants of the Stomach, and various other works designed for the use of children, all of which have attained marked popularity. M. Macé has also been for several years the editor, conjointly with M. Stahl, of the Magazine of Education and Recreation, a semi-monthly journal of great merit.

The work, however, which M. Macé has most at heart is that of popularizing education. With this intent he has for several years been engaged in the work of establishing district libraries in the department of the Upper Rhine, and is now devoting all his energies to the formation of an educational league, designed to promote public instruction in France, and thus to prepare the masses of that noble country for liberty. This league, which is on the highway to success, already numbers thousands of members, each of whom is pledged to do his best to educate the people about him. We trust that we may be pardoned for quoting in this place an extract from a private letter of M. Macé, which will show that the common-school system and the public liberties of the United States is the goal toward which his aspirations tend, and will also set forth the purpose of his efforts. "There is much to be done in this country to fit it for universal suffrage. If you think with me that the friends of human progress should lend each other a helping hand from one land to another, you will perhaps receive with favor a request which I take the liberty of addressing you. We have already on the roll of our league names from England, Germany, Switzerland, Belgium, Italy, and Spain, but none from America. Will you permit me to inscribe yours thereon? You can be of use to our league by making its existence known to the Frenchmen settled in America who still remember their country, and who assuredly desire to see it in the enjoyment of the institutions, and manners and customs of the people amid whom they live. It is to endow them therewith that we are laboring, and many among them doubtless only need to be informed of this to give us their aid."

Meanwhile we are sure that the children of America will feel grateful to M. Macé for the entertainment and instruction contained in the delightful tales which we herewith submit to their perusal.

A 2

THIS TRANSLATION

IS AFFECTIONATELY DEDICATED

To Little Goldielocks,

WITH THE HOPE THAT, LIKE HIS NAMESAKE IN THESE STORIES,

HE MAY INCREASE THE HAPPINESS OF THE WORLD

BY HIS EVERY WORD AND DEED.

CONTENTS.

HOME FAIRY TALES.

LITTLE RAVAGEOT.

I.

Not very long ago there lived a little boy, who was so naughty that every body was afraid of him. He struck his nurse, broke the plates and glasses, made faces at his papa, and was impertinent to his poor mamma, who loved him with all her heart, in spite of his faults. He had been nicknamed Ravageot because he ravaged every thing about him, and he ought to have been very much ashamed of it, for it was the name of a dog, his rival in mischief in the house; but he was ashamed of nothing.

In spite of all this, he was a pretty boy, with light curly hair, and a face that every one liked to look at when he took a fancy to be amiable. But this was never any thing more than a fancy, and the next instant he became unbearable. All the neighbors pitied his parents, who were the best people imaginable, and nothing was talked about

in the whole town but this naughty boy. One
told how Ravageot had thrown a stone at him one
day, when he was taking the fresh air before his
door; another, how he had jumped into the brook
during a heavy rain on purpose to splash the passers-by. The milkman would not let him come
near his tin cans since he had thrown a handful
of fine sand into them through mischief, and the
policeman threatened to put him in prison if he
did not stop pinching the little girls on their way
to school. In short, so much was said of his bad
behavior, that it came to the ears of an old fairy,
who, after long roaming over the world, had taken
up her abode in the neighborhood.

The fairy Good Heart was as good as it was
possible to be; but just on account of her goodness she could not endure evil to be done around
her. The sight of injustice made her ill, and the
mere hearing of a wicked action took away her
appetite for a week. In the course of her long ca-
reer she had punished many bad people, great and
small, and when she learned of all that Ravageot
had done, she resolved to give him a lesson that
would last him a long time. In consequence, she
informed his parents that she would pay them a
visit on a certain day.

The fairy Good Heart was well known in the
country, and every one esteemed it a great honor

to see her enter his house, for she was not lavish of her visits, and it was almost an event when she was seen in the town. On the morning of the day appointed the cook hastened to the market, and returned two hours after, bent double under the weight of a huge basket holding the best that money could buy. The rattling of dishes, and of the old silver plate, taken from great chests, was heard all over the house. Baskets full of bottles were carried up from the cellar, and great hampers of fruit were brought down from the attic. Such a commotion had never before been seen ; the servants were tired out, but no one complained, for all loved the fairy Good Heart, and would have gone through fire and water to please her.

"What shall we do with Ravageot ?" said the father to his wife. "You know how disagreeable he is to people who come here. The unhappy child will disgrace us. If he behaves badly to the fairy every one will know it, and we shall not dare to show our heads."

"Don't be afraid," said the good mother. "I will wash his face, comb his beautiful fair hair that curls so nicely with my gold comb, put on his pretty new blouse and his little buckled shoes, and beg him so hard to be good that he can not refuse me. You will see that, instead of disgracing us, he will do us honor."

She said this because she thought of the good dinner that she was preparing, and she would have been too sorry for her dear little boy not to have been there.   But when the servants went to bring Ravageot to his mother, that she might dress him, he was nowhere to be found.   The naughty boy had heard of the fairy Good Heart, and was afraid of her, without knowing why.   It is the punishment of the wicked to fear every thing that is good.   Hearing himself called, he hid, and was finally found, after a long search, in the pantry, with his fingers in an ice cream that had been set there to keep.   The cook made a great uproar when she saw her beautiful cream spoiled, with which she had taken such pains, but it was in vain to cry out and scold the culprit; the guests were forced to dispense with ice cream for that day.

The worst of the matter was that, in the midst of the cook's lamentations, a great noise was suddenly heard in the street.   It was the fairy Good Heart coming at full gallop.   All the servants rushed at once to the door, leaving Ravageot, who ran and hid among the fagots in the loft.

His poor mother was deeply grieved at not having him by her side on such a day as this; but it was not to be thought of, and, forcing back her tears, she advanced with the most joyful air she

could assume toward the good fairy, who was just
alighting from her carriage, and conducted her
with the greatest respect to the dining-room,
where the whole company took their seats round
a large table magnificently served.

When the repast was ended, the fairy cast her
eyes round the room. "Where is your little boy?"
said she to the mother, in a voice that made her
tremble.

"Alas! madam," replied the latter, "we have had
so much to do this morning that I have not had
time to dress him, and I dare not present him to
you in the state in which he is."

"You are disguising the truth from me," said
the fairy, in a harsh voice, "and you do wrong.
You render children an ill service in seeking to
hide their faults. Bring him to me just as he
is; I wish to see him directly."

The servants sent in search of Ravagcot soon returned, saying that they could find him nowhere.
The father shrugged his shoulders, and the mother began to rejoice in her heart at the thought
that her dear child would escape the lesson that
was evidently in store for him. But the old fairy
did not intend to take all this pains for nothing.
She made a sign to her favorite dwarf, who was
standing behind her chair. This dwarf, who was
called Barbichon, was of the strength of a giant,

despite his small stature. He was broader than he was high, and had long arms twisted and gnarled like the old shoots of the vine. But the most extraordinary thing about him was that he smelt out naughty little boys, and tracked them by their scent as a hound tracks a hare.

Barbichon ran to the kitchen, where Ravageot had been left, and following his scent from there without hesitating, he climbed to the loft and marched straight to the fagots, through which he caught a glimpse of the torn trowsers of the fugitive. Without saying a word, he seized him by the waistband, and carried him at arms' length into the dining-room, where his entrance was greeted with shouts of laughter. Poor Ravageot was in a sad plight. His rumpled blue blouse was blackened on one side by the charcoal in the kitchen, and whitened on the other by the walls that he had been rubbing against ever since morning. From his matted and tangled hair hung twigs and dry leaves, gathered from among the fagots, to say nothing of a great spider's web, through which Barbichon had dragged him on passing through the door of the loft, and half of which was clinging to his head. His face, purple with anger, was daubed with cream from the tip of the nose to the end of the chin. He wriggled and twisted, but in vain, in Barbichon's large hand. In

short, as I just told you, he made a sorry figure,
and those who laughed at him had good reason
for laughing.

Three persons only did not laugh: his father,
whose face showed great vexation, his mother,

whose eyes were full of tears, and the old fairy,
who cast on him a threatening glance.

"Where have you come from, sir?" said she,
"and why did I not see you on entering here?"

Instead of answering, he slipped from the hands

of Barbichon, who had just set him on the floor, ran to his mother, and hid his head in her lap, stamping his foot with anger.

"Here is a child," said the fairy, "that likes to have his own way. Well, I will leave him a parting gift that will render him very happy. HE NEED NEVER DO ANY THING THAT HE DOES NOT WISH. Adieu, madam," said she, addressing the poor mother, who was involuntarily smoothing the disordered hair of her naughty boy with her white hand; "adieu; I pity you for having such a child. If you take my advice, the first thing you will do will be to wash his face, for he is really too dirty." And, rising majestically, she went in search of her carriage, followed by Barbichon bearing the train of her dress.

This was an unhappy household. The fairy Good Heart had gone away displeased, after all the pains that had been taken to entertain her, and the guests disappeared one by one, in haste to tell what had happened through the whole city. The father took his hat and went out angry, saying aloud that this rascal would disgrace them all in the end. The mother wept without saying a word, and continued mechanically to stroke the tangled hair of her dear torment, reflecting on the singular gift that had been made him.

Finally she rose, and, taking Ravageot by the

hand, "Come, my dear little boy," said she, "let us go and do what the fairy bid us."

She took him to her dressing-room, and, plunging her large sponge into the beautiful clear water, prepared to wash his face and hands. Ravageot, still sulky from the reproaches which he had just drawn upon himself, at first made no resistance, but when he felt the cold water in his nose and ears, he began to kick, and ran to the other end of the room, crying,

"Oh! it is too cold; I don't want my face washed."

His mother soon caught him, and passed the sponge over his face again, in spite of his struggles. But the fairy's fatal gift was already at work. The water obeyed Ravageot's orders. To avoid wetting him, it splashed to the right and the left out of the basin, and ran from the sponge, which constantly remained dry, so that it was necessary to give up the undertaking. The room was full of water, while Ravageot's face, half washed, had not received a drop since the imprudent words he had spoken.

His poor mother, in despair, threw herself in a chair, and, shaking her wet dress, said, "Come, let me comb your hair, at least; you will not be quite so untidy." Saying this, she took him on her lap, and began to pass her beautiful gold comb through his hair. Before long the comb encountered a twig, around which five or six hairs were twisted.

"Oh! you hurt me," cried Ravageot. "Let me alone! I don't want my hair combed." And behold! the teeth of the comb bent backward and refused to enter the hair. His mother, frightened, seized another comb, which did the same. The servants of the house hastened thither at her cries, each bringing all his combs, but nothing would do. They even went to the stable in search of the curry-comb; but scarcely had its iron teeth touched the enchanted locks than they bent backward and passed over Ravageot's head without disturbing a single hair.

Ravageot opened his eyes wide, and began to repent of having been so hasty of speech. He was a little vain at heart, and did not dislike to be neat and clean, provided that it cost him neither pain nor trouble. To see himself condemned to remain thus, with his hair full of dirt and his face half washed, was not a pleasant prospect. To show his dissatisfaction, he began to cry with all his might —the usual resource of naughty boys when they know not what to say or to do.

"I want to be washed and to have my hair combed," sobbed he, but it was too late. The fairy had, indeed, exempted him from the necessity of doing what he did not like, but she had not told him that he could do what he pleased.

To comfort him, his mother wished to put on his beautiful new blouse and his pretty buckled shoes. He pushed them away. "I don't want them," he cried. "I want to have my face washed and my hair combed."

As the water would not wash his face, nor the comb enter his hair, after storming a long time, he changed his mind, and asked for his new blouse and buckled shoes. It was the same story. The blouse and the shoes had heard his refusal, and, like well-bred people, refused in their turn to go where they were not wanted. The blouse rose in the air when he attempted to put it on; the higher he raised his hand, the higher it rose, until finally it fastened itself to the ceiling, whence it looked down on him with a mocking air. As to the shoes, the first one that he attempted to put on suddenly became so small that a cat could not have put her paw into it, while the other grew so large that Ravageot might have put both feet into it at once.

His poor mother, seeing this, sent away the servants, who stood wonder-struck, and whose astonishment added to the shame of the little boy; then, gathering her maternal strength to resist the terror that seized her, she gently clasped her poor child to her breast.

"What will become of us, my poor boy," said

she, " if you will not obey at once and without resistance? This is what the good fairy wished to
teach you by her fatal parting gift. *When children are commanded to do any thing, it is for their
good; and the worst thing that could happen to
them would be to have the power to disobey.* You
have this power now, and you see already what it
has cost you. For heaven's sake, watch over yourself henceforth, if you would not kill me, for it
would be impossible for me to live and see you as
miserable as you will soon become, if you continue
to disobey your papa and me."

Ravageot was not a fool, and he perfectly understood the truth of what was said to him. He
loved his mother besides (what child, however
wicked, could do otherwise?), and the profound
and gentle grief of this tender mother softened his
little stony heart in spite of himself. He threw
his arms around her neck, and, laying his dirty face
against her smooth cheeks, wiped away the large
tears that fell silently on it. They alone had the
power to break the enchantment, since he had declared that he would not have his face wet.

The reconciliation effected, they went down
stairs to the room where they usually sat, and there,
on a beautiful polished table, were the books and
copy-books of the little boy.

"Study hard, my dear child," said his mother,

kissing his forehead. "Learn the page which you are to recite to papa this evening like a studious little boy. Perhaps the good fairy will relent when she knows that you have learned it thoroughly, and will take back her vile gift."

If Ravageot had had the choice, he would have gone to play in the garden; but after the humiliating lessons which he had received, one after another, he dared not resist. He seated himself at the table, therefore, and, with a great effort, set to work to learn his page. Unhappily, in the fourth line came a long, hard word, to which he directly took an aversion. This hard word spoiled every thing; it was like a great stone in his path. After uselessly trying several times to spell it, he angrily threw the book on the floor.

"I don't want to study," said he; "I am tired of it."

"Oh!" said his mother, with a look that pierced his heart, "is this what you promised me?"

"Forgive me, mamma," said he, ashamed; and he picked up the book to begin to study his lesson again. It was impossible to open it. His terrified mother used all her strength, but in vain. She called the coachman and the porter—two very strong men—each took hold of one of the covers, and pulled with all his might, but the book did not stir. She sent for the locksmith with his hammer, and the carpenter with his saw; both broke their tools on the book without opening it.

"I will take another," said Ravageot; and he stretched out his hand toward a fairy book that amused him greatly. Alas! it was so firmly glued to the table that he could not stir it. A third disappeared when the little boy attempted to take it, and insolently returned the moment he withdrew his hand. In short, Ravageot had declared that he did not want books; the books no longer wanted Ravageot.

"Ah! unhappy child, what have you done?" exclaimed his mother, in tears. "Now there are no more books for you. How will you ever learn any thing? You are condemned to remain in ignorance all your life." Her tears flowed in such abundance on the unfortunate book, the author of all the evil, that it was wet through, and already, under this all-powerful rain, was beginning to open, when suddenly it remembered its command in time, shook off the tears, and shut with a snap.

Except the book of fairy tales, which he sincerely regretted, Ravageot would have readily resigned himself to being rid of books, for he was not reasonable enough as yet to understand the use of them; but his mother's grief troubled him, and he wept bitterly with her, promising never more to disobey.

Meanwhile, his father returned to supper, worn out with fatigue, and still vexed from the scene at dinner. He had been walking since morning all about the town, avoiding every face that he knew, and fearing to be met, lest he might have to answer questions about the fairy's visit, which was talked of every where; consequently, he was not in the best humor toward the child that had caused him such an affront. I leave you to judge of his anger when he saw his son come to the table with his clothes torn, his hair in disorder, and his face still daubed with half of the morning's cream. Looking at his wife with an angry air, he said, in a loud voice,

"What does this mean, madam? Do you think that we are not yet sufficiently the laughing-stock of the town, that you wait for more visitors to come here before you wash that little wretch?"

The poor woman, seeing her husband so angry, dared not tell him what had happened, and suffered herself to be unjustly accused in order to spare her little boy the punishment that his father might have inflicted upon him, happy that all the anger should fall on her. In this she was wrong again, for the child, full of gratitude to her, was indignant in his heart against his father's injustice, without reflecting that he was the true culprit, and that it was his place, if he had a heart, to justify his mother by telling the truth. The spirit of rebellion once aroused in him, with an appearance of reason, the child set up his will against that good father, whose displeasure was so natural, and he was left in ignorance of what had happened; and when the latter, softening a little, handed him a plate of soup, saying, "Here, eat your supper, child, and afterward we will see about washing you," he answered, in a resolute tone, "I don't want any."

It must be confessed that it was a kind of soup of which he was not very fond, a circumstance which doubtless added something to his resolution. Scarcely had he spoken that unfortunate "I don't want any," when the soup sprang from the plate and fell back with one bound into the tureen, splashing every body around the table.

His father, who had received a large share of the soup on his waistcoat, thought that Ravageot had thrown it in his face. Nothing was too bad for such a child to do. He rose furious, and was about to punish him on the spot, when the mother rushed between them. "Stop, my dear," said she, "the poor child had nothing to do with it. He is unhappy enough without that; now he can eat no more soup." And upon this she was forced to tell Ravageot's father of the fatal power that the fairy had bestowed on him, and to explain the consequences which had already followed from it. As may be imagined, this did not calm him. More angry than ever, he broke into reproaches against his poor wife.

"This is a fine gift," said he; "I congratulate you on it. What is to be done now with this little wretch? The meanest rag-picker would not have him. I want nothing more to do with him, and to-morrow morning I mean to send him as cabin-boy on board a vessel, where he will have to endure more hardships than he will like. Until then, take him away from my sight, and put him to bed; at least, he can do no more mischief in his sleep."

His mother wished to take him away herself for fear of a new accident, but her husband would not hear of it. "No, no," said he, "you will find means of coaxing him, and making him believe that he is an innocent victim. Stay here; Mary Ann shall put him to bed."

Mary Ann was a tall country girl, as fresh as a rose and as strong as a man; she had already received more than one kick from Ravageot, and was not one of his best friends. She took him in her arms without ceremony, and carried him off as if he had been a feather.

Left alone with her husband, the poor mother set to work to caress him and attempt to soften his heart. She at last persuaded him not to send Ravageot to sea as a cabin-boy; but, that it might not be believed that he had yielded to his wife, the father swore solemnly that he pardoned him for the last time, and that he would be merciless at the next offense.

Meanwhile the time passed; half an hour, an hour went by since Ravageot had been carried away, yet Mary Ann did not return. Unable to resist her anxiety, the mother hastened up stairs, when what did she see but Mary Ann clinging to the curtains, and trying with all her might to hold down the bed, which was capering about the room. Vexed at being obliged to go to bed without his supper (for he had not dined, you must remember), the little boy had refused at first to go to bed, and the bed had taken him at his word. As soon as he attempted to approach it, the bedstead reared and plunged like a furious horse; the mattress rose in waves like a stormy sea; and the coverlid itself joined in the dance, and flapped in the face of the disobedient child till it brought tears in his eyes. It was evident that he would have to pass the night in a chair.

It was too much to bear at once. Exasperated by the remembrance of all the misfortunes that had been showered on him like hail ever since morning, he fell into a terrible fit of rage, and roll ed on the floor, gnashing his teeth.

His mother approached him. "Come to my arms, my dear child," said she; "I will wrap my dress about you, and keep you warm all night."

In his fury he listened to nothing, and more than twenty times pushed away the loving arms that offered to shelter him. Worn out at last with crying and struggling, he felt the need of a little rest, and as his good mother still opened her arms, smiling sadly, he sprang toward her to take refuge in them, when suddenly he felt himself held back by an invisible hand, and found it impossible to take a single step forward. It was the final blow. His last disobedience had deprived him forever of the pleasure of embracing his mother.

They passed the night six feet apart, looking at, without being able to touch each other. The poor child was in the greatest terror, and bitterly reproached himself for having scorned the dear refuge which was forever closed to him. But who can tell the despair of his mother? She neither wept nor spoke, but gazed with a haggard face at her child, banished from her arms, and felt that she was on the point of becoming mad.

II.

When morning had come, she said to Ravageot, "Come with me. We will go to the fairy Good Heart, and I will beg her to forgive you."

She attempted to take his hand, but something held her back, and she left the house, followed by the little boy, who no longer had the right to walk by his mother's side.

The fairy Good Heart lived a league from the city, in a great castle surrounded by splendid gardens, which were open to every body. A simple hedge, the height of a man, separated the garden from the road, and the gate was always on the latch. Ravageot and his mother had no trouble, therefore, in making their way to the fairy. Before the door they found Barbichon, taking the fresh air, and waiting for his mistress to rise. The good lady was not a very early riser; it was a little fault in which she indulged herself in return for doing harm to no one. But as soon as she learned that some one was waiting to see her, she sprang from her bed, and was ready to receive the afflicted mother in the twinkling of an eye.

"Ah! madam," said the latter, as soon as she saw the fairy, "ah, madam, save us! For pity's sake, take back the terrible gift which you made yesterday to my child."

"I see what is the matter," said the fairy, glancing at Ravageot's dress. "This little boy wished to have his own way. He has been punished for it; so much the worse for him. I can not take back what I have given."

"What!" said the mother, "is there no means, then, of saving him from so frightful a punishment?"

"There is, but it is a hard one. It is necessary that some one should consent to be punished in his place."

"Ah! if that is all, it is easy. I am all ready. What do you ask for him to be able to have his face washed, and be neat and clean?"

"For him to have his face washed, and be neat and clean, you must give me your beautiful complexion."

"Take my complexion, madam; what do I want of it, if my child must always remain untidy?"

Barbichon instantly stepped forward, holding in one hand a basin of rock crystal, and in the other a sponge as soft and fine as velvet. In the twinkling of an eye, the fairy washed the face of Ravageot, who smiled to see himself in the glass, fresh and rosy. But all his joy vanished when he turned to look at his mother. Her beautiful cheeks were withered, and her smooth, satin-like skin was tanned and wrinkled like an old woman's. She did not seem to perceive it, and her eyes sparkled with pleasure on gazing at her dear child.

"What do you ask," she continued, "for him to be able to have his beautiful hair combed and curled?"

"For him to have his hair combed and curled, I must have your hair."

"Take my hair, madam. What do I want of it, if my dear child's must always remain in disorder?"

And Barbichon stepped forward with a diamond comb, with which the fairy, with three turns of the hand, smoothed and curled the hair of Ravageot, who let her do it without daring to look at his mother. When he ventured to raise his eyes to her, his heart was wrung with pain. Her beautiful hair, as black and glossy as jet, had disappeared, and in its place a few gray locks strayed in disorder from her cap. But she paid no attention to it. "What do you ask," she continued, "for him to be able to put on his new clothes?"

"For him to put on his new clothes, I must have yours."

"Take my clothes, madam. What do I want of them, if my dear child must always remain in rags?"

Barbichon instantly handed the fairy a little jacket of fine cloth, embroidered with gold, white silk trowsers, a blue velvet cap, trimmed with silver, and shoes ornamented with precious stones, which in two seconds replaced the old clothes of Ravageot. He had never been so fine. He could not repress a cry of joy, which quickly turned to one of sorrow; for, on looking at his poor mother, he saw her dressed in rags like a beggar. But she saw nothing but the magnificent costume of her child, and laughed with pleasure, showing her magnificent pearly teeth, the last relic of her past beauty.

"What do you ask," she said, "for him to be able to eat soup? The doctor says that his health depends on it."

"For him to eat soup, I must have your teeth."

"Take my teeth, madam. What do I want of them, if my dear child can not have proper nourishment?"

She had scarcely finished, when Barbichon held on an enameled plate a beautiful Japanese cup, in which was smoking the most appetizing soup that ever smoked under a little boy's nostrils. Ravageot, who had been fasting for twenty-four hours, did not wait for the spoon to be offered him twice: but his pleasure was of short duration. At each spoonful that he swallowed he heard a tooth fall on the ground. Despite his hunger, he would have gladly stopped; but his mother, delighted to see him eat with such an appetite, would not listen to it, and forced him to go on till not a tooth remained in her head.

"Now," said the fairy, "this is all, I hope."

"All! oh no, madam, I have many more things to ask of you."

"But, unhappy woman, what more would you sacrifice for this naughty child?"

"They are not sacrifices. I am too happy to save him from the wretched fate that was in store for him. Come, what do you ask for him to be able to sleep in his bed?"

"For him to sleep in his bed, you must give me yours."

"Take my bed, madam. What do I want of it, if my dear child must pass his nights on the hard floor?"

"Have you any thing more to ask?"

"Yes, indeed. What do you ask for him to be able to study?"

"For him to be able to study, you must your-self forget all that you know."

"Take all I know, madam. What do I want of knowledge, if my dear child must wallow in ig-norance?"

"Let this be your last demand, at least."

"For heaven's sake, one more! This time it is for myself. What do you ask for me to be able to clasp him in my arms?"

"To have the happiness of clasping him in your arms, you must give me all your other happiness."

"Take it, madam. What other happiness can there be for me, if I have not that of embracing my dear child?"

The fairy made a gesture, and Ravageot sprang tremblingly into his mother's arms. He shuddered in spite of himself as he came in contact with her coarse dress and yellow, flabby skin, and winced under the kisses of her toothless mouth. But so many proofs of love had not been lost on him, and all that excited his repugnance filled him at the same time with gratitude and admiration for the good mother who had so completely devoted herself for him, to what point he did not yet know. As to her, wholly absorbed in the happiness which she had restored to him, she clasped him convulsively in her arms, and never tired of telling him how handsome he was, forgetting all that she herself had lost.

It was necessary at last to take leave. The happy mother could not sufficiently thank her whom she styled her benefactress. Barbichon wept with emotion, and the fairy herself, unable any longer to restrain her feelings, ran to her as she was descending the first step, and kissed her forehead, saying, "Take courage, noble woman, and rely on me."

Courage! she was too happy to need it. She walked with a light step, holding by the hand her treasure, well fed, neat and clean, and adorned like a little prince. What mattered any thing else to her? She thought that he would sleep that night in his comfortable little bed, and pictured to herself in advance how learned he would be one day, and how he would write a beautiful book, which the first publisher of the country would print on fine paper, with his name on the title-page in large letters.

Meanwhile the poor mother knew nothing herself, as she soon saw when they set out for home. She had forgotten the way; she did not even know the direction of the town, and had not the least recollection of the house. Ravageot then understood the full extent of her sacrifice. It was in vain that he attempted to guide her. He had been too much accustomed to have every thing done for him to take the trouble to see where he was going, and had paid no attention to any thing on his way. They wandered about all day in the fields; he growing more and more anxious as night came on, she thinking of nothing but the happiness of seeing her dear child delivered from all his ills.

At last, toward evening, they were met by the servants, whom his papa, terrified at their disappearance, had sent in search of them in all directions, and who did not recognize them at first, so much were they both changed, until Ravageot, who was looking anxiously on all sides, spied the coachman. He ran to him, and, calling him by name, soon made himself known; but he was greatly embarrassed when the servants asked who was the old beggar woman with him. "It is my mother!" he exclaimed. But they laughed in his face, and the policeman, who headed the search, scolded him severely for roaming over the country, clinging to the skirts of a wretched old woman, and calling her his mother—he whose mother was such a lady. They even talked of taking her to prison. She knew not how to defend herself, having forgotten every thing; she only clasped Ravageot in her arms, repeating, "He is my son, my dear son, whom I have saved from misery. Nothing in the world can take him from me."

Happily they thought her insane, and, respecting her madness, permitted her at last to accompany Ravageot to his father. It was dark when they arrived. Mary Ann was standing at the door.

"Ah! here you are," she cried, as soon as she saw the little troop. "Here you are, naughty boy! Your father has been anxious enough about you, poor man! He has just gone to the great pond to look for you. This is the third horse he has tired out since morning, and if it had not been for your dear mother, whom we all love so well, I should have advised him to remain quiet, and thank God for being rid of you. What have you done with your mother?"

"Here she is!" cried Ravageot, trembling with terror at the turn affairs were taking. "Here she is; I have never left her."

"No more of your tricks! Aren't you ashamed of them at such a time? How can you make fun of your mother in this way, when you see us all in trouble on her account? Up stairs with you, quick, and to bed! You must be in need of it."

At the word bed the good mother remembered her bargain with the fairy, and put an end to the discussion by saying, "Go to bed, my dear; you know that the fairy permits it, and you must be very tired. Sleep sweetly, and I will wait for you here."

He wished to resist, but she raised a finger, and said, in her beautiful voice, which remained clear and sweet, "Obey!"

At this word a thousand terrible recollections rose before him. He hung his head and followed Mary Ann, who dragged him up stairs less gently than he would have liked.

Ravageot was in his comfortable little bed,

wrapped in his warm blankets, but he slept little. He thought of his mother standing and waiting for him before the door—his mother disfigured on his account, whom no one would recognize, and who so cruelly expiated the faults which he had committed. He listened with terror to the sound of the rain and the roaring of the wind, which blew that night with extraordinary violence. The rattling of the windows, shaken by the tempest, seemed to him so many accusing words, crying, "Bad son!" At last, toward morning, worn out with fatigue and excitement, he fell into a heavy, painful sleep, and saw in a dream a squad of policemen driving before them a gray-haired woman, in a coarse patched gown, who turned her head as if looking for some one.

Meanwhile his father had returned late at night, worn out, with a heart full of anxiety. He received the news that his son was found with a cry of joy; but on learning that his wife was not with him, he groaned, and, throwing himself on the sofa, passed the night there, with his face buried in his hands. Scarcely had day dawned when he entered the room where his son was sleeping, and, seeing the little curly head which he had thought never more to behold, he burst into tears like a child, and rushing to the bed, covered the little sleeper with kisses

Ravageot awakened with a start, and was at first terrified to see his father drowned in tears, but soon recovering himself, he threw his arms round his neck, and cried, " Oh ! papa, mamma is down stairs at the door. Come quickly ; I am sure that she is very cold." And as his father looked at him wonderstruck, " They did not know her yesterday," cried he, " but you will know her, I am certain."

Hastily dressing himself, he dragged his father to the door, where they found the poor woman, her cheeks blue with cold, and her clothes dripping with rain. At the sight of her little boy her face brightened, and she clasped him in her arms with as complete a happiness as if she had been receiving the compliments of the fine gentlemen of the town in her great velvet chair by the drawing-room fire.

" What does this mean ?" said the father; "who is this good woman ?"

" It is my mother," cried the child—" my good mother, who has become ugly and ragged for me."

" Can this be possible ?" said he to his wife; " and are you really my dear wife, for whom I have been mourning ever since yesterday ?"

She looked at him without recognizing him. She embraced her child again, and said, " This is my son. What do you want of me ?"

" But then I am your husband!" returned the father, stupefied.

" You!" said she. " I do not know."

" Oh! what am I to believe?" cried the unhappy man. " This is really my wife's voice, but I do not know her or she me."

At this moment Mary Ann, who had been awakened by hearing her master walking about the house, arrived. She seized her mistress by the arm, and, shaking her rudely, exclaimed, " Are you here yet? Begone, child-stealer, and never let us see your face again."

She was attempting to drag her to the street, when Ravageot madly threw himself on her. His little heart swelled with anger, and he would have marched boldly at that moment against a battalion of soldiers.

" No!" he exclaimed, beside himself, " you shall not drive mamma away. I do not want what she has done for me. It is for me to be dirty, and to sleep on the ground; I am the one that has deserved it. Take me back to the fairy! I will give her back every thing, and she must give back every thing to mamma."

He had not done speaking when an enormous hand seized Mary Ann by the waist and sent her spinning in the middle of the street, and Barbichon exclaimed, " Make way for my mistress!"

At the same instant the fairy Good Heart rose
from the ground, and, placing her hand on the
shoulder of the tender mother, "Your trial is ended," she said. "She who did the evil has come
to repair it."

Then she kissed Ravageot on both cheeks, and
disappeared with Barbichon, leaving after her a
sweet odor that lasted for a week.

When the father, recovered from his surprise at
this sudden apparition, raised his eyes to his wife,
he saw her, with her beautiful black hair and her
fresh complexion, in the silk dress which he had
bought himself for her birthday. She looked at
him, and they fell into each other's arms with un-
speakable happiness.

She lived afterward happy and honored, respected like a saint by all the town; but when
any one attempted to speak in her presence of her
sublime devotion, she blushed and changed the
subject.

As for Ravageot, he became from that day the
best-behaved little boy that ever was seen. He
obeyed without speaking, and gave up his wishes as soon as they displeased his father or mother. He was never more heard to complain when
the water was cold, or to cry when his hair was
combed, or to refuse soup when there was something else on the table that he liked better.

However early his mother saw fit to put him to bed, he took care never to refuse to go, for fear of the consequences. He attended to his studies, remembering at what a price his mother had thought it worth while to redeem them for him, and would have thought it a crime to run from her when she wished to take him in her arms. In this manner he soon lost the name of Ravageot, and was called good little Ernest, the name that his parents had given him in baptism.

C

GOLDIELOCKS.

THERE was once a good little boy, who liked to see every body happy. He had large blue eyes, fair, rosy skin, and such beautiful golden hair that he was known throughout the whole country by the name of Little Goldielocks. He often mourned because he was too weak and too small to be of any use in the world, and if he felt in haste to be a man, it was only that he might have the power of doing good. There are not many little children of this sort, it is true. Goldielocks is a proof, however, that there are some such.

At that time there lived a great magician, an intimate friend of the good fairies, who corresponded with him from the four quarters of the globe. This correspondence was very easy. Each of them had an enchanted box, with a little hole in the top. They wrote what they had to say on a bit of paper, and slipped it into the hole, when lo! the paper went straight to its address, alone by itself, without any farther trouble. You can understand how convenient this was, and how easy it was for the magician to know all that was going on in the world.

In this way he found out what was troubling Goldielocks, and he was so deeply affected by it that he instantly felt himself growing better, that is to say, more powerful; for you must know that he belonged to a class of magicians whose power was in exact proportion to their goodness.

"Ah!" cried he, "this child thinks himself too weak, yet he has made me stronger than I was before. I must give him some aid." And, putting on his spectacles, with which he could see a thousand miles, he looked toward the house where the little boy lived. It was quite a nice house, lost among the multitude of houses in a long street. The street itself was confounded in the magnitude of a large city, which, however, was not the most important one in the country, and the country, in its turn, although of considerable size, was only a speck on the globe. I leave you to imagine what a small place the little boy held in it.

Goldielocks at that moment was seated alone in the nursery, with a book in his hand that did not seem to amuse him much, watching his sisters, who were merrily picking strawberries in the garden for their mamma. It was the day for making sweetmeats, and the whole house was in commotion about such an important event. It must be confessed that Goldielocks was a little indolent, as the magician saw at once from the way in which he held his book, which was oftenest bottom upward. He was evidently thinking less about his lesson than the sweetmeats. The little boy could not keep his feet still a single minute; and had been delighted to hear somebody say one day in his presence that birds and little children should be suffered to hop and skip about as much as they pleased, because God made them for it. He had no scruples, therefore, in leaving the tiresome book every few moments to go to play with two beautiful Canary birds, his rivals in skipping about, whose cage, suspended from the wall, was one of the chief ornaments of the room; or else to pay a visit to his garden, a great pot of earth, in which he and his sisters had planted some orange-seeds the winter before, and which now held orange-trees three inches high, a thousand times more tenderly cared for than those of kings in their orangeries. This did not seem calculated to make much effect on the world.

"I will make this dear little fellow the most important personage on earth," said the great magician. "Every time that he wins a victory over himself, all mankind shall do the same."

Then, turning his telescope in a different direction, he went to see what was taking place in a

gigantic palace, where a great meeting of states-
men was solemnly discussing what color the
queen's dress should be on her coronation day.

Goldielocks held in his little hands, therefore,
without knowing it, the destinies of the whole
human race. He learned his lesson no better on
that account. Seeing that his orange-trees were
a little dry, he had just finished gently sprinkling
a glass of water over them, when a darling little
fairy, who had undertaken to make a man of him,
entered the room without knocking.

"Well!" said she, somewhat vexed, "is this the
way that you learn your lesson?"

"Oh! I could not leave our trees in this condi-
tion; they were dying of thirst. And besides, I
have been studying my lesson a long time."

"Well, recite it, then."

He did not know a word of it.

"My little Goldielocks, you make me very sad," said the fairy, as she quitted the room, wiping away a tear.

The child began to reflect, and, ashamed of his conduct, he sat down to his book, and studied it courageously, without paying the least attention to any thing else. His feet were still for a little while, in spite of the example set by the Canary birds, who were not made to study—poor little

creatures! In a quarter of an hour the lesson was well learned, and Goldielocks, enchanted with himself, ran in search of the good fairy to recite it to her.

Meanwhile a great change had taken place on the globe. All the little truants who were wandering about the streets left their marbles and mud pies, and ran to school as fast as their legs could carry them. The ignorant became ashamed of their lack of knowledge, and the booksellers, suddenly besieged by the impatient crowd that filled their shops, knew not where to find books enough to satisfy so many demands at once. Those who knew nothing were seized with an impulse to learn something; those who knew something felt the need of learning more; there was a general revolution in minds—the happiest that had been seen since the beginning of the century—and Goldielocks had done this all alone by learning his lesson well.

He was rewarded personally by a warm kiss on each cheek, and, the time for luncheon having come, he was invited to take part in a splendid feast, composed of a beautiful pyramid of slices of bread spread with the strawberries that had escaped the preserving-kettle. A lady who took a great interest in the children of the family had sent them a pot full of cream, and there was a universal cry of admiration when the group found themselves in the presence of all these good things. Nothing gives one such an appetite as hard work. Goldielocks, who was no glutton, nevertheless stretched his hand with pleasure toward a fine slice of bread from the part of the loaf that he liked best. Happy and proud of having learned his lesson well, he chattered as he ate, and carefully laid aside the finest strawberries to eat last with his cream. His little brother, whose appetite knew no bounds, had devoured the whole of his before Goldielocks was half through luncheon. The little fellow looked with a wishful eye at his brother's bread, large strawberries and saucer of cream, and determined to have them. As he was as willful as he could be, a scene of cries and tears would have followed had not Goldielocks, touched with compassion, divided with the poor hungry child, though he would have gladly eaten the whole. His mamma, who had arrived on the spot meanwhile, was greatly delighted, and gave Goldielocks a smile that amply repaid him for his sacrifice.

But he had a far greater reward; for lo! at the same instant, all over the globe, men suddenly began to reflect how many of their fellow-beings might be famishing with want, and each one set out with provisions in search of the hungry. Nothing was seen in the streets but baskets filled with bread, great platters of meat, sacks of potatoes, and baskets of fruit, on the way to the houses of the poor. Every one who was fortunate enough to find a family in want, loaded it with plenty, and his neighbors envied him his happiness. The suffering poor could not believe their eyes. Children who had never seen any cake in their lives made the acquaintance of that remarkable product of human industry, and — a thing that had never before been seen—no one on that day went supperless to bed.

What a triumph for Goldielocks! But he knew nothing of it. For a full quarter of an hour he was wholly absorbed in a great question. The little fellow was very pretty—at least he had often been told so by his nurse, who worshiped him, and who had no greater happiness than that of dressing him in his fine clothes. After luncheon, a walk in the large garden, where all the rich children were in the habit of meeting, was talked of, and every one ran to get ready. Now Goldielocks had a black velvet coat, in which he thought himself dazzling. His nurse was of the same opinion, and, though the velvet coat had been designed for holidays, she never lost an opportunity to take it from the drawer. His mamma then scolded, but the mischief was done, and the child strutted about like a peacock. This time, again, the nurse brought out his velvet coat, which was joyfully received. He already had one arm in the sleeve when his elder sister entered. "Oh! Goldielocks," she exclaimed, "you mustn't wear that coat. Your cloth jacket is good enough to play in the dirt."

"My cloth jacket has holes in the elbows. I look like a beggar in it."

"Come, be good; you know that mamma will be displeased."

The dear little boy said no more; the idea of displeasing his mother made him forget all his vanity. He took off the coat, and quietly put on the cloth jacket, in which he amused himself like a king in the garden.

He had scarcely obeyed his sister when Pride instantly took flight from the earth. Great ladies in damask robes began politely to return the salute of the humblest citizens. The noblemen of the court found themselves saying good-morning to the peasants whom they met returning from market. Men tried to remember the reasons which they had had for despising each other, but were unable to find them. You can form no idea of the universal relief. Even the little boys that had stood first at school were rid of the foolish pride which had rendered them so ridiculous.

What was Goldielocks doing all this time?

On his return from his walk, a great dispute had arisen between him and one of his sisters, only a year older than himself, whom, nevertheless, he loved with all his heart. Alice, for that was her name, had a fault common to all little girls—she was something of a tease. Her brother having said before her several times that he meant to be a physician, she called him nothing but doctor, and during the whole walk she had tormented him with this hateful name.

"I am tired of being a doctor," said poor Goldielocks, at last. "I mean to be a bishop."

This was much worse, and the name of My Lord the Bishop began to be showered upon him.

"When are we to ask My Lord the Bishop for his blessing," said she at last, bowing before him with feigned humility.

"You shall have it directly," cried Goldielocks, furious; and, seizing a ruler that lay close at hand, he began to make the most threatening gestures toward the provoking Alice.

Alice, whose hands were as nimble as her tongue, quickly found another ruler, and the two champions began skirmishing with all their skill, taking care, however, to strike, not each other, but the piece of wood in their adversary's hand. An unlucky blow, however, having fallen on Alice's fingers, she uttered a cry of pain, which made Goldielocks forget his anger. He dropped the ruler, and, throwing his arms round his sister's neck,

"Forgive me," he cried, with tears in his eyes; "I will never do so again, and you may call me bishop as much as you like."

Their papa, who was the best papa in the world, had hastened toward them at the noise of the quarrel, and was already preparing to scold, when what was his joy to see the brother and sister tenderly embracing each other. He clasped them to his heart, and thought himself a happy man in having such good children.

Great wars were raging at that moment upon the earth, and men were striving which should invent the most frightful engines of destruction. Some had constructed iron towers, moving faster than a horse could gallop, and filled with men, who, sheltered from danger, could kill without fear all whom they met. Others had invented engines which could hurl huge rocks two leagues, and kill soldiers by thousands like flies. Each new invention called forth bursts of applause from the combatants, and there would have soon been no one left alive but the inventors of machines for killing had not Goldielocks' blessed ruler encountered Alice's fingers.

The child had no sooner laid down his arms than all this warlike ardor ceased as if by enchantment. Men instantly perceived that it was very foolish to kill each other to know which was right. It was agreed to refer the disputes to the lookers-on; and there was a universal embracing all along the lines, from the generals to the chil-

dren of the common soldiers, who had been in the habit of fighting whenever they met on their way from school.

Good little Goldielocks went to bed that night content with his day, after receiving a thousand caresses from his family, and fell asleep, asking himself when he would be as large and strong as a man. At the same moment the earth, delivered by him from ignorance, want, pride, and war, abandoned itself to transports of universal joy; and from Norway to Patagonia great bonfires were kindled on all the mountains, which blazed so brightly that they could have been seen from the moon.

The great magician is no longer at hand, my dear children, to give such importance to the victories which you win over yourselves. Something remains of it, however; even to-day, believe me, children are stronger than men in doing good. While your parents are sometimes obliged to make the greatest sacrifices to prevent you from being unhappy, you, on your side, can render them happy by the smallest sacrifices. If the world is not changed in a single moment thereby, as in the time of Goldiclocks, be sure that these petty sacrifices are never lost on it. Every drop of water that falls finds its way to the sea.

BIBI, BABA, AND BOBO.

Bibi was a little mischief.

Baba was a little glutton.

And Bobo was a little sluggard.

They went one day to walk in a wood that was near their house, and, in spite of their parents' orders, did not stop at a certain place, beyond which they had been forbidden ever to go. I must add that they were three disobedient little girls into the bargain.

It is only just to say that this was Bibi's fault. On reaching the place, Bobo already felt tired, and would have been glad to stop. Baba, on her side, recollected that luncheon would be ready in half an hour, and did not care about going any farther. But Bibi, who was above such trifles, laughed so much at the other two that they dared not resist her. One was ashamed of her indolence, and the other of her gluttony, and both followed Bibi, though sorely against their will. This will teach you how weak you are when you undertake to obey through any other motive than obedience; for if our little girls had thought of

nothing but their parents' wish that they should
not go beyond this spot, they would have felt in
themselves that they were right, and would not
have been afraid of being laughed at.

They went on, however. It was a large and
beautiful wood, crossed by magnificent roads that
stretched as far as the eye could reach. The
walk at first was delightful. The children gathered flowers, rolled on the soft grass, and listened
to the chirping of the birds. Sometimes a little
mouse put the end of his nose out of a hole, and
drew it in as soon as the little girls came too
near; or a great gray lizard sprang suddenly
from a tuft of grass and ran along the road,
chased by the merry group.

Every thing went on well as long as they remained in the road, which was as straight as an
arrow, and in which there was no danger of getting lost. But by-and-by they reached a shady
footpath which wound among the thicket, and
which looked so inviting that Bibi entered it
boldly.

"Don't go that way; we shall lose ourselves,"
cried Bobo.

"Let us go back; it is time that we were
home," cried Baba.

"I am only going to the first turning," answered Bibi. "Come with me; I must see what is
beyond it."

And, as they turned a deaf ear to her entreaties, the mischievous little girl threw herself on the ground.

"Oh! what a nice place to lie down in," she cried, "and how thick the strawberries are!" On hearing this they ran to her—Baba, the gourmand, to eat strawberries, and Bobo, the sluggard, to lie on the grass at her ease. But the soft spot was full of stones and dead branches, and as for strawberries there was not one. Bibi burst into a loud fit of laughter on seeing their disappointed faces. "We shall find them farther on," said she to Baba; and, taking her hand, she dragged her forward as fast as she could, followed at a distance by Bobo, who had a great mind to cry.

After the first turning there came a second, which she insisted on seeing, and then a third. Then the footpath parted in two, and a gigantic oak, which rose in the bushes on the edge of one of the paths, attracted Miss Bibi's attention. From one caprice to another, she led Baba and Bobo so far that when they wished to retrace their footsteps none of them knew which way to go.

The poor children were filled with consternation. Bibi, however, would not show it. She stamped her foot, pinched her lips, opened her black eyes wide, and, turning with a contemptuous gesture toward her companions, "Follow me, you little frightened chickens," said she, "and I will lead you home."

But it is not enough, in a wood, to be determined to go somewhere; it is necessary, also, to know the way. After walking a long time, trying all the footpaths, and passing and repassing the same places, they were just where they were at the beginning. Bobo at last threw herself on the ground, and declared, crying, that she could not take another step. She was a beautiful little child, with fair complexion, golden curls, and large blue eyes, with a pleading expression, which would have moved a heart of stone, but which did not touch the teasing Bibi, who shook her, and tried to raise her from the ground. Poor Bobo did not defend herself, but fell back with all her weight on the grass after each attempt.

"You are a fine walker!" cried Bibi. "We will leave you here if you have not more courage."

But Baba came to the aid of her friend. "Don't be afraid, dear Bobo," said she; "I will not leave you. Rest yourself, and then we will set out again:" and, bending her good-natured, chubby face, she kissed her friend to give her courage.

"If I only had a little piece of bread," murmured she, "I would wait as long as you like," and she heaved a deep sigh. Bobo looked at her with compassion. Just at that moment her eyes fell on a beautiful ripe strawberry, shining lusciously among the leaves a few steps from her. It was the first that they had met. Forgetting her fatigue, she rose at once and ran to the strawberry, which she brought back in triumph to poor hungry Baba.

"Oh! how good it is," said the latter, swallowing it. "Thank you, Bobo; you are a good girl."

In the mean time Bibi, to show her superiority, was walking backward and forward with long strides. Baba's joy displeased her. "A fine dinner for a glutton!" she cried; "it will not carry you far."

This was unhappily but too true. Suddenly recalled to the consciousness of her situation, and feeling her appetite redoubled rather than appeased by the delicious but unsatisfactory mouthful, the poor child burst into tears, and Bobo, on seeing her, began to sob to keep her company, while Bibi laughed like the naughty girl that she was.

Just at that moment the queen of the fairies passed by and heard them. She had been chosen queen by the other fairies because she was the best of them all, and so good that she had compassion on every one in trouble, even the wicked.

She suddenly appeared to the children in the form of an old woman laden with a bundle of dry fagots. "What is the matter, my dears?" said she. "Can I help you in any way?"

"Oh! madam," said Bobo, "poor Baba is so hungry."

"That is not all," said Baba; "poor Bobo is so tired. We have lost our way in the woods, and know not how to get home."

The good fairy looked at them attentively, and saw what they had done.

"Be comforted," she said; "I will send you some aid."

She broke two little twigs from her fagots, and threw them into the thicket, when instantly a great white sheep, with a fleece like snow, came out bleating, and rubbed his nose on Baba's rosy cheeks; then a beautiful little squirrel leaped from a tree without ceremony upon Bobo's shoulder.

"And you, my little one," said the old woman, addressing Bibi, "are you in want of nothing?"

"No, mother," answered Bibi, with a haughty air, "I am neither hungry nor tired. They make me laugh with their complaints."

"Ah! you ask for nothing but to laugh," said the good fairy, irritated at the tone of the little girl. "Very well; I have something that will satisfy you."

She instantly vanished, and behold! a little monkey appeared, which gamboled before Bibi, making the drollest grimaces that could be imagined. Delighted with her gift, Bibi took him in her arms, and covered him with kisses, to which he replied by a short, angry growl. She paid no attention to that, however, so amusing and delightful did he seem to her.

All this did not bring the children any nearer home. Baba ran her fingers through the silky wool of her sheep, dreaming of a slice of bread and marmalade, which she saw dancing before her eyes, while Bobo kissed her squirrel's whiskers, without really knowing what she was doing.

The mistress of the sheep, being the most impatient, was the first to speak. "Now," said she, " how are we to get home?"

"Don't trouble yourself," said the sheep; "I know the way."

He began to trot slowly in the right direction, followed by his little mistress, who gave her arm to Bobo, telling her to lean upon it.

Bibi attempted at first to laugh at them, and took another path, saying that she did not mean to be led by a sheep; but the monkey having escaped from her arms, she was forced to run after him, and as he obstinately persisted in following the band, she at last resigned herself to necessity, and walked behind her companions, sneering at them continually, and calling them all sorts of names.

On the way, Baba, who never lost sight of her fixed idea, loudly complained and cried of hunger. "Mr. Sheep," said she, "can't you show me any thing good to eat here?"

"I can teach you, my pretty child," answered Colas, for that was his name, "not to be so fond of eating, and to learn to silence your stomach when an accident happens like that of to-day. What would become of me if I did not know how to be hungry in case of need—of me, who am driven out into the highways to feed on the blades of grass growing among the stones?"

"But at least," resumed Baba, "you have something to eat."

"Yes, but never to my taste. I do not complain, however, because it can not be helped. Follow my example, and acquire the habit of courage against necessity. You will sup all the better for not having dined."

Baba was not convinced, but she no longer dared complain before so reasonable an animal. She talked of something else with Colas, who conversed so agreeably that she soon lost sight of that seductive slice of bread and marmalade which had constantly appeared before her, and the sight of which had made her so unhappy

Meanwhile Bobo had also entered into conversation with her squirrel, whose name was Cascaret, as he told her directly. She told him how her limbs ached, how her feet were blistered, and how she was sure that it would make her ill.

"My dear little mistress," said Cascaret, cocking his tail above his head like a bunch of feathers, "I believe that by ceasing to think of your fatigue you would feel it less. You see how slender I am, and how delicate my limbs are. They are far more tender than yours; yet that does not hinder me from nimbly leaping among the branches, which is much more tiresome than walking quietly on the ground. Come, run with me; it will rest you."

"Oh no," said Bobo, groaning, "I do not think so."

"There are some beautiful nuts up yonder," said the squirrel, "and a great wild apple-tree full of fruit, which will soon be stolen if the little boys come this way."

"Oh! how fortunate," cried Bobo, delighted. "My dear Cascaret, won't you be so good as to bring me some apples and nuts for poor Baba, who is so hungry?"

Master Cascaret did not wait for a second bidding. He sprang forth nimbly, and made so many journeys to the walnut and apple trees

that Baba finally declared herself quite satisfied.
Bobo felt so much pleasure in seeing her eat that
she almost forgot her fatigue, and walked on
without paying any attention to it.

An idea struck Baba in turn. "Mr. Sheep,"
said she, "will you do me a great favor?"

"What?" said Colas.

"Will you take my dear Bobo on your broad
back? I am sure that she will be quite safe on
your thick wool, and she is so light that she will
not tire you much."

The sheep was too good-natured to refuse. He
knelt down, and Bobo, clinging to his fleece, soon
found herself seated like a little queen on the
good Colas, who trotted on as if he had no load.
Thanks to their mutual kindness, the two friends
were both freed from their suffering. They were
no longer afraid of losing themselves, since the

good sheep) knew the way, and they continued
their journey, merrily talking and singing.

Bibi followed them, making faces at the monkey, which pinched and bit her without ceremony,
but with such comical and original grimaces that
she shouted with laughter. At length, however,
she began to grow tired of a play that was
amusing only on one side, and gradually approached the singers. The beautiful nuts and
yellow apples, which she had seen Baba and Bobo
eating, had reminded her that she had eaten nothing for a long time, and she began to feel that
she would not be sorry to have something herself to munch. She at last determined to have
recourse to her whom she had treated so harshly.

"Where is your squirrel?" said she to Bobo.
"Can't he bring me some fruit too?"

Bobo, who was not revengeful, whispered a
word in Cascaret's ear, and the good little animal
climbed like lightning into a great walnut-tree
that had sprung up as if by magic in the midst
of the wood. He returned with a large nut,
from which he carefully stripped the green husk,
then cracked it with his long front teeth, and
gracefully offered it with his right paw to Bibi.
Just as she was stretching out her hand to take
it, the mischievous monkey sprang forward, and,
seizing the nut, ran a few steps before his mis-

tress; then, standing on his hind legs, he ate the nut before her face, rolling his eyes and twisting his mouth as if wishing to defy her. A second nut shared the same fate; and the little girl having succeeded in seizing the third, the monkey snatched it from her hands before she had tasted it.

She was forced to abandon all thoughts of profiting by Bobo's kindness; but, as she felt herself overcome by fatigue in consequence of all this vexation, she asked permission at least to seat herself on the sheep's back. Colas willingly consented. He knelt down for Bibi to change places with Bobo; but, just as she had taken her seat, the mischievous monkey sprang on the gentle sheep, and pulled his ears with such force that he began to leap and rear madly. Miss Bibi fell her whole length on the ground among the briers, and scratched her face and hands so badly that she did not ask to mount again, but dragged her weary limbs along in the rear of the party, feeling more like crying than laughing.

Happily, they soon reached the end of the wood. Colas took a footpath, and, at the moment when they least expected it, the little girls suddenly saw their parents' house before them. Baba and Bobo rushed forward with cries of joy, while Colas and Cascaret gamboled round them, to show the share that they took in their happiness.

The little monkey remained seated at the edge of the wood, gazing at Bibi, who hobbled along, too sorrowful and tired to follow the example of the others. Missing him from her side, she turned round to call him, and saw him scratching his head with a careless air. She ran to him, furious. "Are you laughing at me again?" she cried. "You naughty little animal, you are good for nothing but mischief. Take care, or I shall punish you at last."

He would have been whipped soundly could she have caught him; but he sprang aside, and suddenly turned into a beautiful woman magnificently dressed, with a wand in her hand. It was the queen of the fairies herself, who had assumed this disguise in order to show the little mischief all the deformity of her ugly fault.

"Now," said the fairy, "I hope that you understand how much you put yourself beneath others by laughing at them. Your friends have their faults, which they will do well to reform; but they have a good heart, and goodness makes amends for every thing. You see that they have succeeded in extricating themselves from their difficulties, while you, who thought yourself far superior to them, because you had more wit and spirit, return last, famished and exhausted with fatigue. Whenever you feel like amusing yourself at the expense of others, remember the little monkey that you saw just now, and as you hated him, think that they will hate you."

The child was humbled, but not conquered, for her heart rebelled against the fairy's words, and she saw nothing but the shame which would be cast on her by this adventure.

"They are going home each with a beautiful gift," said she, "and I shall have nothing."

"No, my child," resumed the good fairy, "I will make you a present worth a thousand times as much as theirs."

And, taking Bibi in her arms, she clasped her to her heart overflowing with goodness. The little girl felt her own instantly melt, like an icicle placed over the fire. She returned home with a good heart, and from that day henceforth she employed her courageous spirit in strengthening and assisting the weak, instead of teasing and laughing at them. And in after years, when she herself was a mother, she would say to her children, "Every one has his faults, but never forget, my dears, that that of teasing others is, perhaps, the worst of all."

D 2

MISS CARELESS.

Miss Careless was a good little girl, who loved her papa and mamma dearly, but, as her name shows, she had one bad fault—she took no care of any thing. When her parents scolded her she hung her head, her large blue eyes filled with tears, and she looked so lovely and so unhappy that they almost reproached themselves for having given her pain, and involuntarily set to work to comfort her; but, their backs turned, all traces of repentance disappeared, and the disorder became worse than ever.

Careless had a brother a year older than herself, whose example and advice had a bad influence over her. It was the custom in that country, when boys had hardly begun to cut their second teeth—at the age when it is so pleasant to hear them prattling about the house in their pretty frocks, with their long curls falling over their shoulders—it was the custom, I say, to send them to great houses, built like barracks, where, after cropping their heads, they were dressed in military coats buttoned to the chin, patent-leather

belts, and soldiers' caps perched over the ear, lack
ing nothing but swords to be equipped for battle.
The poor children learned there to play men, and
to look down on their sisters. It was a thing
agreed upon in this little world that a man who
respects himself puts nothing in its place, and the
example of the most celebrated personages, re-
nowned for their absent-mindedness, who always
put on their trowsers wrong side before, was
quoted as a proof of genius. The grown persons
of the house had told this to the tall lads, who
had told it to the smaller boys, who had told it
to the little ones, and Careless's brother, who was
one of the latter, had repeated it to her.

Armed with this imposing testimony, Careless
thought it very absurd to require of her such
minute attention to details so insignificant, and
nothing seemed to her so tiresome as to put
things in order one day which must be disturbed
the next. She did not suspect what need she
would have of order in after years, when she
should become a mother herself, and how disgrace-
ful it is to a woman to have nothing in its place
in her house. Her mamma, who was well acquainted with her faults, and who loved her too
well to suffer this fatal habit to become rooted in
her, knew not what to do to break her of it; she
had exhausted every thing — warnings, prayers,

threats, and even tears, and she finally resolved to punish her.

It was not a difficult task to punish the dear little girl; her heart was so tender that a harsh look made her unhappy, and the sight of her mother in tears threw her in despair. Unhappily, all this sorrow was wasted, since she would not feel the importance of what was required of her. It always seemed to her that her parents were very wrong in making such a fuss about things that were so little worth the trouble, and that they made her unhappy without rhyme or reason. They were obliged, therefore, to have recourse to more direct punishments, in order to make a stronger impression on her mind. If her bed was in disorder, she was forced to wear her nightcap all day. Every time she overturned her inkstand, and this often happened, the end of her nose was inked. Whenever she left a handkerchief, or any thing else, lying about the house, it was fastened on her back; I even believe that a shoe was hung there one day, which had been found far from its fellow, astray on the stairs.

All this mortified her greatly, but did not reform her. She finally persuaded herself, indeed, that her parents no longer loved her, since they persisted in tormenting her in this way, and this unhappy thought hardened her in her disorderly habits. One day, at length, when her brother had a holiday, and, between them, they had put every thing out of place in the parlor and dining-room, Miss Careless was told that she must not leave her room all the next morning. This was a punishment which she felt keenly, for the young gentleman's presence was a rare event since he had joined the regiment, and he now introduced into their plays those cavalier and domineering airs which rendered him still larger in the eyes of his little sister. The dear child was too good.

The next morning the rising sun found her seated on her bed in tears, looking despairingly about her room, her prison till dinner. Her pretty new dress, put on for the first time the night before in compliment to her brother's arrival, was thrown in a corner, half on the floor and half on a chair. One of her boots was under the door, and the other against the door. Two pretty gray silk mitts were on each end of the mantle-piece, and the little black velvet hat, of which she had been so proud, was lying on its side on the top of the water pitcher, with its great white plume falling into the basin.

Careless saw all this confusion with profound indifference, and only thought how tiresome it would be to stay alone for long hours in a room with nothing to do, since it did not occur to her to put things in order.

"How unhappy I am!" she cried. "Every one here hates me, and treats me badly. Nobody loves me but my dear Paul, and they won't let me play with him."

The fairy Order was at that moment making her rounds through the house. She had always avoided this neglected room, for she had a profound contempt for giddy and negligent little girls, and the young lady was not one of her favorites; but when she heard her gentle voice moaning so pitifully, she had compassion on her, and, believing that she had repented at last, opened the door.

You may imagine how she frowned at the sight of the disorder. "Are you not ashamed?" she exclaimed, harshly, advancing to the foot of the bed.

"Of what, madam?" answered the little girl, tremblingly.

"Just take the trouble to look around this room."

"Well, what is the matter with it?"

"What! don't you see the frightful disorder that every thing is in? There is not a single article of your dress in its place."

"Oh! if that is all, there is no great harm

done.   Paul says that it makes no difference where we put our things at night, provided that we find them in the morning."

"So you believe Master Paul, and think that it makes no difference where you put your things!" cried the fairy, angrily.   "Well, you shall see."

With these words she touched the child with her wand, and behold! little Careless flew into pieces in every direction.   The head went in search of the hat on the water-pitcher, the body plunged into the dress across the chair, each foot regained its boot, the one under the bed and the other against the door, and the hands made their way into the mitts on each end of the mantle-piece: it was the work of an instant.

"Now," said the fairy, "I am going to send Master Paul to put all this in order.   You shall see whether it makes no difference where you put things."

She went down into the court-yard, where Master Paul was taking advantage of his mamma's absence to try to smoke the end of a cigar that his papa had forgotten the night before.   "Go up stairs to your sister's room," said she: "she needs you."

Paul was not very sorry to be disturbed in an attempt which he was beginning to find unpleasant; nevertheless, he carefully laid the precious cigar-stump on the window-sill, and went to his sister's room, his head somewhat heavy.

"Well, what is the matter?" said he on entering. He saw no one in the room. "Where are you?" he cried, furious at what he thought a trick insulting to his dignity.

"Here," groaned the head. "Come and help me quickly, my dear Paul; I am very uncomfortable on this water-pitcher."

"No, come here," howled the body. "I can't bear this any longer; the corner of the chair is piercing me through and through."

"Don't leave me under the bed," said the right foot.

"Look against the door," said the left foot.

"Don't forget us on the mantle-piece," shouted the hands, with all their might.

Another little boy might have been frightened, but Paul was already strong-minded. Picking up the feet, hands, and head in the twinkling of an eye, "Don't be alarmed, my dear sister," said he, in an important tone; "I will set you to rights; it will not take me long. The deuce!"

This was one of his words, borrowed from a friend that had taken him under his protection, a young man of eleven, who had long since renounced the refinement of good language. Yet it was not six months, since, seated on his mam-

ma's knee every evening before going to bed,
with his hands clasped, he had promised God to
be a good boy. But we will return to the work
of putting together the scattered limbs of poor
Careless.

The feet, head, and hands were soon laid by
the side of the body, and, as Master Paul had
said, the operation was quickly performed. Raising his sister on her feet, "There you are!" he exclaimed.

But scarcely had he looked at his work than
he uttered a loud cry. The head was turned

awry; one of the feet, in its boot, hung on the left arm, while one leg staggered, supported by a poor little hand that looked as if it were crushed beneath the weight.

"Oh! Paul, what have you done?" cried the unhappy Careless. And as she attempted to wipe her eyes, the toe of her boot caught in the braids of her hair.

The giddy boy stood thunderstruck before the disaster which he had caused. He attempted at first to repair the evil by pulling his sister's head with all his might to put it in the right place;

but it was too firmly fixed. He twisted the little girl's neck in every direction, and only succeeded in making her cry. Then fright and grief triumphed over all his courage, and he burst into a good hearty fit of crying, like a genuine little boy. The servants of the house ran thither at his screams, but they could think of no other remedy than to send for a physician. Some proposed Doctor Pancratius, who had cured so many little children; others the celebrated Doctor Cut-all, who knew so well how to perform an operation. Every body talked at once, and they were trembling for fear of the arrival of the parents, whom such a sight might have brought to the tomb, when the fairy Order appeared in the middle of the room in all the lustre of her holiday attire.

"Well," said she to the poor little girl, "do you think now that it makes no difference where you put things, and that children are to be trusted who despise order? Let this be a lesson to you! I forgive you because you are a good girl, whom every body loves; but always remember what it may cost you to pay no attention to what you are doing."

Saying this, the fairy touched her once more with her wand, and head, body, feet, and hands found their right places.

After this terrible adventure the little girl became so careful and attentive that the fairy Order made her her favorite, and married her in after years to a prince as beautiful as the day, who was anxious above every thing to see his house in perfect order, and who chose her as much for her neatness in all things as for her goodness and beautiful face.

As to Paul, he ceased to believe that it made no difference where he put things, and refused to listen to the boys, on his return to school, when they made speeches that would have displeased his mamma.

THE NECKLACE OF TRUTH.

THERE was once a little girl by the name of Coralie, who took pleasure in telling falsehoods. Some children think very little of not speaking the truth, and a small falsehood, or a great one in case of necessity, that saves them from a duty or a punishment, procures them a pleasure or gratifies their self-love, seems to them the most allowable thing in the world. Now Coralie was one of this sort. The truth was a thing of which she had no idea, and any excuse was good to her provided that it was believed. Her parents were for a long time deceived by her stories; but they saw at last that she was telling them what was not true, and from that moment they had not the least confidence in any thing that she said. It is a terrible thing for parents not to be able to believe their children's words. It would be better almost to have no children, for the habit of lying, early acquired, may lead them in after years to the most shameful crimes, and what parent can help trembling at the thought that he may be bringing up his children to dishonor?

E

After vainly trying every means to reform her, Coralie's parents resolved to take her to the enchanter Merlin, who was celebrated at that time over all the globe, and who was the greatest friend of truth that ever lived. For this reason, little children that were in the habit of telling falsehoods were brought to him from all directions, in order that he might cure them.

The enchanter Merlin lived in a glass palace, the walls of which were transparent, and never in his whole life had the idea crossed his mind of disguising one of his actions, of causing others to believe what was not true, or even of suffering them to believe it by being silent when he might have spoken. He knew liars by their odor a league off; and when Coralie approached the palace, he was obliged to burn vinegar to prevent himself from being ill.

Coralie's mother, with a beating heart, undertook to explain the vile disease which had attacked her daughter, and blushingly commenced a confused speech, rendered misty by shame, when Merlin stopped her short.

"I know what is the matter, my good lady," said he. "I felt your daughter's approach long ago. She is one of the greatest liars in the world, and she has made me very uncomfortable."

The parents perceived that fame had not de

ceived them in praising the skill of the enchanter, and Coralie, covered with confusion, knew not where to hide her head. She took refuge under the apron of her mother, who sheltered her as well as she could, terrified at the turn affairs were taking, while her father stood before her to protect her at all risks. They were very anxious that their child should be cured, but they wished her cured gently and without hurting her.

" Don't be afraid," said Merlin, seeing their terror ; " I do not employ violence in curing these diseases. I am only going to make Coralie a beautiful present, which I think will not displease her."

He opened a drawer, and took from it a magnificent amethyst necklace, beautifully set, with a diamond clasp of dazzling lustre. He put it on Coralie's neck, and, dismissing the parents with a friendly gesture, " Go, good people," said he, " and have no more anxiety. Your daughter carries with her a sure guardian of the truth."

Coralie, flushed with pleasure, was hastily retreating, delighted at having escaped so easily, when Merlin called her back.

" In a year," said he, looking at her sternly, " I shall come for my necklace. Till that time I forbid you to take it off for a single instant; if you dare to do so, woe be unto you!"

"Oh, I ask nothing better than always to wear it, it is so beautiful."

In order that you may know, I will tell you that this necklace was none other than the famous Necklace of Truth, so much talked of in ancient books, which unveiled every species of falsehood.

The day after Coralie returned home she was sent to school. As she had long been absent, all the little girls crowded round her, as always happens in such cases. There was a general cry of admiration at the sight of the necklace.

"Where did it come from? And where did you get it?" was asked on all sides.

In those days, for any one to say that he had been to the enchanter Merlin's was to tell the whole story. Coralie took good care not to betray herself in this way.

"I was sick for a long time," said she, boldly, "and, on my recovery, my parents gave me this beautiful necklace."

A loud cry rose from all at once. The diamonds of the clasp, which had shot forth so brilliant a light, had suddenly become dim, and were turned to coarse glass.

"Well, yes, I have been sick! What are you making such a fuss about?"

At this second falsehood the amethysts, in turn, changed to ugly yellow stones. A new cry arose.

Coralie, seeing all eyes fixed on her necklace, looked that way herself, and was struck with terror.

"I have been to the enchanter Merlin's," said she, humbly, understanding from what direction the blow came, and not daring to persist in her falsehood.

Scarcely had she confessed the truth when the necklace recovered all its beauty; but the loud bursts of laughter that sounded around her mortified her to such a degree that she felt the need of saying something to retrieve her reputation.

"You do very wrong to laugh," said she, "for he treated us with the greatest possible respect. He sent his carriage to meet us at the next town, and you have no idea what a splendid carriage it was—six white horses, pink satin cushions with gold tassels, to say nothing of the negro coachman with his hair powdered, and the three tall footmen behind! When we reached his palace, which is all of jasper and porphyry, he came to meet us at the vestibule, and led us to the dining-room, where stood a table covered with things that I will not name to you, because you never even heard speak of them. There was, in the first place—"

The laughter, which had been suppressed with great difficulty ever since she commenced this fine story, became at that moment so boisterous that

she stopped in amazement; and, casting her eyes
once more on the unlucky necklace, she shuddered
anew. At each detail that she had invented, the
necklace had become longer and longer, until it
already dragged on the ground.

"You are stretching the truth," cried the little
girls.

"Well, I confess it; we went on foot, and only
staid five minutes."

The necklace instantly shrunk to its proper
size.

"And the necklace—the necklace—where did
it come from?"

"He gave it to me without saying a word,
probabl—"

She had not time to finish. The fatal necklace
grew shorter and shorter, till it choked her terribly, and she gasped for want of breath.

"You are keeping back part of the truth," cried
her school-fellows.

She hastened to alter the broken words while
she could still speak.

"He said—that I was—one of the greatest—
liars—in the world."

Instantly freed from the pressure that was
strangling her, she continued to cry with pain
and mortification.

"That was why he gave me the necklace. He

said that it was a guardian of the truth, and I have been a great fool to be proud of it. Now I am in a fine position!"

Her little companions had compassion on her grief, for they were good girls, and they reflected how they should feel in her place. You can imagine, indeed, that it was somewhat embarrassing for a girl to know that she could never more pervert the truth.

"You are very good," said one of them. "If I were in your place, I should soon send back the necklace: handsome as it is, it is a great deal too troublesome. What hinders you from taking it off?"

Poor Coralie was silent, but the stones began to dance up and down, and to make a terrible clatter.

"There is something that you have not told us," said the little girls, their merriment restored by this extraordinary dance.

"I like to wear it."

The diamonds and amethysts danced and clattered worse than ever.

"There is a reason which you are hiding from us."

"Well, since I can conceal nothing from you, he forbade me to take it off, under penalty of some great calamity."

You can imagine that with a companion of this kind, which turned dull whenever the wearer did not tell the truth, which grew longer whenever she added to it, which shrunk whenever she subtracted from it, and which danced and clattered whenever she was silent—a companion, moreover, of which she could not rid herself, it was impossible even for the most hardened liar not to keep closely to the truth. When Coralie once was fully convinced that falsehood was useless, and that it would be instantly discovered, it was not difficult for her to abandon it. The consequence was, that when she became accustomed always to tell the truth, she found herself so happy in it —she felt her conscience so light and her mind so calm, that she began to abhor falsehood for its own sake, and the necklace had nothing more to do. Long before the year had passed, therefore, Merlin came for his necklace, which he needed for another child that was addicted to lying, and which, thanks to his art, he knew was of no more use to Coralie.

No one can tell me what has become of this wonderful Necklace of Truth: but it is thought that Merlin's heirs hid it after his death, for fear of the ravages that it might cause on earth. You can imagine what a calamity it would be to many people—I do not speak only of children—if they

were forced to wear it. Some travelers who
have returned from Central Africa declare that
they have seen it on the neck of a negro king,
who knew not how to lie, but they have never
been able to prove their words. Search is still
being made for it, however, and if I were a little
child in the habit of telling falsehoods, I should
not feel quite sure that it might not some day be
found again.

E 2

FRIQUET AND FRIQUETTE.*

FRIQUET loved his little sister dearly, but he knew no greater pleasure than that of teasing her. Friquette also loved her brother, but she never let slip an opportunity of playing a trick on him. This was the cause of continual pouting, tears, fits of anger, and, I am ashamed to say, even blows and scratches, which are always wicked, but much worse between brother and sister. The naughty children did not understand how much pain they were giving their mamma, who was so anxious to see them constantly happy and good-humored, and who often wept in secret at the sorrow caused her by their conduct.

I must tell you the true cause of all these disputes. Master Friquet was proud of being a man, and fancied that, holding this high position, a little girl had no right to oppose him. Friquette, on her side, had heard it said that men should always give way to ladies, and, being a lady, wished to take advantage of this privilege. It was difficult for two such opposite pretensions

* Pronounced *Fré-kay* and *Fré-ket*.

to exist side by side, so that the brother and sister, while really loving each other at heart, lived like cat and dog.

Friquet was a stout boy, with great fists, and the strength was on his side. Friquette was a little girl, delicate, shrewd, and cunning, who always had the advantage in the end through her wit, of which she had enough and to spare. I will not tell you all the naughty tricks they played each other; unkindness between brother and sister is something so sad that I should take no pleasure in telling or you in hearing it.

You must know, however, that one spring morning, when the children were in the garden with their mamma, the thought struck Friquette to ask for a bit of ground that she might make a garden of her own, and this being instantly given her, Friquet insisted on having one too, not because he had a great desire for it, but in order not to have less than his sister. One of the chief sources of their quarrels was this wicked feeling of jealousy, which did not permit one to witness the pleasure of the other without envying, instead of rejoicing at it. Children with a good heart know nothing of this feeling, and, by way of reward, the happiness of others makes them happy, while it makes the jealous miserable, who have only what they deserve.

To return to Master Friquet: scarcely had the gardens been partitioned off than he ran to the gardener's lodge, where some light tools were kept for the use of his grandpapa, who amused himself from time to time by working in the flower-beds. A little spade, a little hoe, a little rake, even to a little pointed dibble, which his grandpapa used to put the tulip bulbs into the earth—in the twinkling of an eye he took possession of the whole, and, laying his booty on the ground, would not allow poor Friquette to come near it. It was in vain for her to beg; he turned a deaf ear to her; and when she succeeded in seizing one of the tools while his back was turned, it was of little advantage to her, for he snatched it rudely from her hands. I have sometimes seen little boys treat their sisters in this brutal way, and I well remember that they have always been sorry for it.

This time Friquette's spite punished the rude boy, which was really no better, for spite is as bad as rudeness. Their mamma, who had been sent for to see a visitor, had left the garden; and the little girl, left defenseless before her despot, was compelled to drag painfully to her garden a great spade almost as heavy as herself, with which she strove to turn up the ground as well as she could, all the time planning how to revenge herself. Meanwhile Friquet, fully provided with all he needed, soon spaded, raked, and prepared a beautiful bed, and began to talk already about planting it.

"I will go for the seeds," said Friquette, springing toward the house, and leaving him astonished at such obligingness.

The cunning little girl listened to every thing that was said before her, and remembered all that she heard. Now she had heard her father say one day at the table, while talking of gardening, that seeds exposed to too great heat lose the power of taking root, and, when put into the ground, do not produce flowers or vegetables any more than if they were pebbles. She ran to the drawer where the seeds were kept, took out what she wanted, and returned with several packages neatly tied up and labeled, which she gave Friquet. She took good care not to tell him, however, that, before returning to the garden, she had gone to the kitchen, which had happened for a moment to be empty, and had left the packages for five minutes in the oven by the side of the meat that was roasting for dinner. They were a little scorched, indeed, but he did not notice it.

"Thank you," said Friquet, who wished to return her politeness. "Don't you want me to plant some in your garden?"

"Oh no, it is not ready yet, and this spade tires me too much. I have had enough of gardening for to-day." Saying this, she returned to the house to laugh at her ease, while Friquet carefully planted his seeds in rows, and artistically grouped the flowers which must infallibly bloom in a garden so well dug up.

Friquette had a beautiful doll, the confidante of all her joys and sorrows, a model friend that never thwarted her, that remained where she was placed, and that always listened to what she said. It is not worth the trouble of playing a trick without having some one to whom to tell it. As soon as she reached the house, Friquette took her doll in her arms, and, in order not to be disturbed, carried her to an upper chamber where the linen was kept. She stood her against one of the great presses, and, seating herself in front of her on a little stool, began to tell her the story of the garden, with so many details, and adorned with such fine comments, that never was doll harangued in so interesting a fashion.

Meanwhile Friquet had buried every one of his precious seeds in the ground. Nothing remained for him but to wait for the flowers, and, beginning to find it dull to be alone, he determined to ask his sister to join him in some other play. There was not much variety in their amusements, it must be confessed. Sometimes they played horse, and it was naturally he that held the whip. Sometimes they played robber, and, as the one in authority, it was he again naturally that took the part of policeman. Sometimes they undertook a game of hide-and-seek, but it did not usually last long, for he always insisted on being the one to hide, and this invariably caused a rebellion in the end. In consequence of his well-known habits, his sister was not very fond of these games, and when she heard him calling Friquette! Friquette! all over the house, she did not stir, but quietly continued her conversation with her beloved doll.

By prowling about, the young gardener finally made his way to the linen-room, and great was his indignation against the rebel who preferred the company of a doll to the honor of playing with him. With one bound he sprang upon his little rival, and ran with it around the room, triumphantly waving it over his head. But this was a subject on which Friquette would bear no jesting. She was like a lioness whose young are attacked: she chased the robber round the room, trying to frighten him with her screams, and threatening him with her little sharp nails, with which he had already been made acquainted. Friquet, on his side, was as nimble as a monkey.

Seeing himself too closely pressed, he leaped upon a table that stood against the linen-press, drew a chair toward him, sprang upon it, and in less time than it takes to tell the story, stood on the top of the press, uttering a cry of victory, and rubbing the doll's nose against the ceiling.

Friquette was beside herself, but she did not lose her presence of mind. In the twinkling of an eye, she carried off the chair, pushed away the table with a strength which anger alone could have given her, and behold! Friquet was left a prisoner on his perch, in close company with the ceiling, and unable to escape. Seeing him at her mercy, she bitterly reproached him for his conduct, and, in the warmth of her discourse, somehow let slip the fatal secret which reduced all his hopes to nothingness. She had at first intended to keep this to herself, in order to enjoy the pleasure of seeing him look for the flowers every day, and carefully pluck up the weeds that might injure them; but the anger of little girls is so impetuous as to sweep away all calculation, however well laid it may be, and in this the dear little creatures are better than we—their imprudence redeems their malignity.

Friquet foamed with rage on learning the horrible truth, but what was he to do? His enemy knew but too well that she was out of his reach;

she replied to his imprecations by a disdainful gesture, and majestically quitted the room, leaving him to his wretched fate.

He soon gained his freedom, for he began such a hubbub, howling with all his might, and kicking the sides of the linen-press, that the whole house shook. His mamma ran thither affrighted, followed by the old lady who was visiting her, and who thought that something terrible must have happened. They both burst out laughing on seeing the bird on his perch, and, by means of a step-ladder, soon restored him his liberty.

"What were you doing up there, my poor Friquet?" asked the old lady.

The child tried to speak, but his voice was choked with shame and anger. His mother had ceased to laugh on seeing his gloomy and dejected face; she saw that it was another of his sister's tricks, and was filled with profound sorrow. She took the poor boy on her lap, and tried to soothe him by gentle words and tender kisses, and to learn what had happened, but he refused to speak, and ground his teeth silently with rage.

"I see that we must bring Miss Friquette," said the old lady, setting out in search of the culprit.

This lady was none other than the celebrated

fairy Blanchette, so called because her hair had grown white at a very early age, a sign of premature wisdom. The fairy Blanchette possessed the inestimable gift of being able to reform naughty children. She saw at a glance the cause of all the evil, and they knew not how to resist her eye. It must also be said that she loved them with all her heart, which gave her a great advantage over them, for the most rebellious child easily suffers himself to be subdued by a firm will, when he feels that there is love behind it. As to love, mothers always have enough of it and to spare: but the will is not invariably in the foreground. And then Blanchette was a fairy, which explains every thing.

She soon appeared, holding the little girl by the hand, and set her face to face with her brother, whom she did not approach without fear.

"What have you been doing?" asked the fairy, in a harsh voice.

"He took my doll and spoiled it."

"No," cried Friquet, suddenly finding his tongue, "she roasted the seeds in the oven, and then gave them to me to plant, so that nothing might grow in my garden."

"Why did you take all the tools yourself, and rub the skin off my hand in snatching the little spade from me?"

And the two children, becoming animated at the story of their wrongs, glared at each other, clenching their fists, and looking like two cocks ready to fight.

"Let me alone," said the fairy. She took the little boy and held him in the air as high as her arm could reach. Then she raised the little girl from the ground in the same manner, looking at them tenderly, after which she placed them both in their mamma's lap, and kissed her forehead, "Farewell, my dear lady," said she; "be of good cheer; you will see me again in a year from this time." As she quitted the room, she turned toward the children and said, "Above all things, I forbid you to tell a word of it to any one."

Tell what? You would never guess.

Friquet looked at himself: he had on a little dress and an apron trimmed with ribbons, and golden curls were floating over his shoulders.

Friquette had on a blouse, confined by a belt, and a pair of trowsers; and on putting her hand to her head, she found her cropped hair covered with a cap.

A glance in the tall mirror at the end of the room revealed to them the change. Friquet had become the little girl, and Friquette the little boy. The former mechanically opened and shut his hands, which had become small and delicate;

and, finding that he had lost his usual strength, he was humbled. The latter felt her brain duller than usual, and was not less humbled at the loss of her quickness of thought.

Seized with common despair, they threw themselves weeping into each other's arms, mutually embracing the image of what they had been; while the poor comforted mother hoped for happier days, seeing that the fairy's charm was beginning to take effect on them. Without asking for the explanation which they had been forbidden to give, she enjoyed this happy change, and covered them with caresses which they timidly returned.

In the mean time their papa came home to dinner. He was a great mathematician, who was consulted on difficult questions for a hundred leagues around; not one of those flippant scholars whose theories are overthrown with a breath, but a substantial, ruddy, square-set man, with a formidable voice, and eyes that glittered like carbuncles. He would have been taken for an ill-tempered man had he not had a heart of gold, which gave his face an expression of goodness to those who knew how to read it.

When the good man returned at evening, his head confused with algebra and geometry, the thought of the merry little faces waiting for him at home made the blood circulate warmly through his veins; the heart again took the lead of the head; from a scholar he became a kind and loving father, and he reached his door with a smiling face, eager to forget the tiresome brain-work of the day in the prattle of his children. But, alas! on entering, how often he found sullen faces and swollen eyes. His eyes then flashed like lightning; he spoke in his gruffest tones; he scolded his wife herself when she tried to interfere, and began to cross-question the children with merciless severity. But the little rogues knew his weak point, and when they succeeded in wheedling him into a smile, were it but for a second, he was lost. Then began a cross-fire of accusations, loud contradictions, and explanations which explained nothing; and, far from resting, the poor father saw problems on his hands to be solved far more complicated than those over which he had toiled all day, with pen or chalk in hand. You see how wrong it was for children thus to destroy the few moments of repose of so good and learned a father.

"Well," said he, throwing himself angrily in a chair, "what is the matter now?"

"Friquet has been naughty," said the little boy.

"No, no, Friquette has been bad," said the lit-

They had forgotten, at the sight of their father, that they had changed their habitations, and each one hastened to excuse the former tenant. This was a new thing for the father, who was not accustomed to such self-denial.

"Very well," said he, relenting; "you are good children, at last, to accuse yourselves. Come, tell me the whole story, my darlings."

And, overjoyed at being able to embrace them at his ease, he lifted them both with one arm and seated them on his knees, where he danced them while waiting to hear the story of their crimes.

Friquette, a little boy, and Friquet, a little girl, reflected in the mean time what they should do. They were forbidden to tell of the metamorphosis, and, moreover, who would have believed them? To justify themselves in their former character was to accuse themselves in the new one, and to call down punishment on their own heads. On the other hand, the accusing cry that had heedlessly escaped the lips of the false Friquet and Friquette had been so well received by coming in the shape of a confession that it was very encouraging.

Friquet, who had the more readiness of thought since he had become a little girl, was the first to decide what course to take. He told how the boy had abused his strength in the garden, and how he had ran away with the doll in the linen-room; but he naturally took good care not to dwell on the details, leaving in the shade those that were the most unfavorable, and even mentioning the extenuating circumstances. It was really touching, for those who did not know the secret of the farce, to see the sister showing such caution in blaming the brother; while the father, wonder-struck, took advantage of the opportunity to embrace them both once more.

Then came Friquette's turn. Her tongue was less ready than usual; nevertheless, she acquitted herself tolerably well. She told the story of the seeds in her gentlest voice, with her eyes cast down, and on glancing sideways to see whether her papa was very angry, to her great surprise she saw him smiling with delight. God has made it a fixed law with mothers and fathers that they shall admire their children, so that we all, whatever we may be, shall be admired at least once in our lives; and, faithful to this gentle law, the good scholar completely lost sight of the blackness of the malignity, and was in ecstacies at having a daughter so learned for her age.

"What! you little monkey, do you know that already?" he exclaimed, stroking the silky hair that now covered the head of Master Friquet.

"How did you find that out? Do you hear, my dear? Here is a child six years old learning vegetable physiology all alone by herself."

"I know nothing about your vegetable physiology," answered his wife, "but I know that here are at least ten cents' worth of seeds wasted."

"No matter, we will buy some more. Well, little doctor in petticoats, since you know so much, tell me how many degrees of heat were needed to make your experiment succeed."

This Friquet did not know. He had gained all the wit of his sister, but what was stored in her memory she had carried away with her. He did like children that I have seen in school: he moved his lips, but said nothing.

The poor mother had to bear the blame. "See! you have frightened the poor child with your ten cents," said the husband. "I am sure that she knows."

"Friquette had heard that it needed two hundred and twelve degrees," said the little boy.

"Do you hear? They both know. You are two darling children; let me kiss you." Never was there a happier father, and it is needless to add that no more was said about the quarrels of the day.

Friquet and Friquette grew familiar with their new position on seeing that every thing went on so well. The next morning, when their parents went into the garden, their eyes filled with tears of joy at the sight of their boy vigorously digging up Friquette's piece of ground, and their little girl bending over Friquet's bed, carefully planting new seeds. It was at first through old associations that they rendered each other these little services which gave their parents such pleasure, but the habit soon became so pleasant to them that they continued through kindness what they had begun through selfishness. The boy employed his strength for his sister, and the girl her wit for her brother, without thinking of their own interests, for the one was as happy in doing the service as the other was in receiving it. In the end, they no longer remembered which was Friquet and which Friquette, and when the fairy Blanchette came according to her promise at the end of the year to set things right again, neither seemed to care for it, for they had but one heart between them.

You may imagine what a welcome the good fairy received in this household from which she had driven disputes, ill-nature, and tears, and how warmly she was greeted by the parents, whose life had been a season of continual rejoicing since they had had such good children, and who, strange as it may seem, loved each other much better than before. No one suspects how much coldness naughty children often cause between their papa and mamma by the disagreements to which they give rise. The poor mathematician, who had formerly found so little rest at home from his weary labors, now returned in peace to his little paradise. He no longer suffered from rush of blood to the head, and never was in bad humor. The mother, who was already beginning to grow thin and pale through grief at her children's conduct, again became fresh and rosy now that she was happy all day long.

They told the fairy Blanchette, with a thousand expressions of gratitude, how much joy they had in their children, and what pleasure they felt in seeing them, when they took them on a holiday to the menagerie, walk hand in hand, talking lovingly together, and showing each other little marks of kindness; how the little boy would take his sister in his arms and hold her up to gain a better view of the animals, while the little girl, who remembered every thing, would tell her brother their names.

"But what was it that you did to the children when you raised them from the ground?" asked the mother.

"I taught them, my dear friend, to live each other's lives, and to place their happiness and

pride outside their little selves; I destroyed selfishness in them by making them understand that
it is to our interest to be kind to others.   What
I did is not difficult; every one can do the same."

"Ah!" said the father, who thought of other
things besides mathematics, "why can not some
good fairy like you be found also to lift from the
earth so many grown children who are eying
each other with hostile looks, and to send them
to live in each other's places, were it but an hour
in the year—how many quarrels between breth-
ren would speedily be ended on the globe!

MEDIO POLLITO.

Medio Pollito, a Bantam pullet, by labor and frugality once saved a hundred crowns. The king, who is always in want of money, had no sooner heard of it than he sent to borrow them, and Medio Pollito was proud to lend her money to the king. But there came a bad season, when she would have been very glad to have it again. She wrote letter after letter to the king and the ministers, but no one replied, so that at last she resolved to go in search of her money herself, and set out for the king's palace.

On the way she met a fox.

"Where are you going, Medio Pollito?" said he.

"I am going to see the king, who owes me a hundred crowns."

"Take me with you."

"It will not be the least trouble. Jump down my throat, and I will carry you."

The fox jumped down her throat as he was bid, and on she went, delighted at having done him a favor.

A little farther on she met a wolf.

"Where are you going, Medio Pollito?" said he.

"I am going to see the king, who owes me a hundred crowns."

"Take me with you."

"With pleasure. Jump down my throat, and I will carry you."

The wolf jumped down her throat, and off she went once more. He was a little heavy, but the thought that he wished to make the journey gave her courage.

As she drew near the palace she met a river.

"Where are you going, Medio Pollito?" asked the river.

"I am going to see the king, who owes me a hundred crowns."

"Take me with you."

"I have a heavy load already; but, if you can find room down my throat, I will carry you."

The river made itself very small, and glided down her throat on the spot.

The poor little chicken could scarcely walk, but she managed to reach the door of the palace. Rap, rap, rap, went the knocker. The porter put his head out of the window to see who was there.

"Whom do you want to see, Medio Pollito?" said he.

"I want to see the king, who owes me a hund-red crowns."

The porter took pity on the innocent young chicken. "Go away, my pretty pullet," said he. "The king doesn't like to be disturbed, and those who trouble him have to suffer for it."

"Open the door," said she. "I must speak to the king. He is well acquainted with me; he has my property."

The king was told that Medio Pollito wished to speak with him. He was at the table, feasting with his courtiers. He burst out laughing, for he suspected what was the matter.

"Bring in my dear friend," said he, "and put her in the poultry-yard."

The door opened, and the king's dear friend entered quietly, persuaded that she was about to receive her money. But, instead of taking her up the great staircase, the servant led her to a little court-yard, raised a latch, and behold! Medio Pollito found herself shut up in the poultry-yard.

The cock, who was busy with a lettuce leaf, looked down on her without saying a word; but the hens began to peck her, and to chase her in all directions. Hens are always cruel to strangers that come to them unprotected.

Medio Pollito, who was a peaceful and orderly little chicken, not accustomed to quarreling at home, was terribly frightened at the sight of all these enemies. She crouched in a corner, and cried with all her might.

"Fox, fox, come out of my throat, or I am a little lost chicken!"

And behold! the fox jumped out of her throat, and ate up all the hens.

The servant who carried the corn to the poultry found nothing but feathers on her arrival. She ran in tears to tell the king, who turned red with anger.

"Shut up this crazy Medio Pollito in the sheep-fold," said he; and, to comfort himself, he ordered some more wine.

Once in the sheepfold, Medio Pollito saw herself in greater peril than in the poultry-yard. The sheep were huddled close together, and threatened every moment to trample the poor chicken under foot. She had just succeeded in taking shelter behind a post, when a great ram threw himself down there, and nearly smothered her in his fleece.

"Wolf, wolf, come out of my throat, or I am a little lost chicken!" cried she.

And behold! the wolf jumped out of her throat, and slaughtered all the sheep in the twinkling of an eye.

The king's anger knew no bounds when he learned what had just happened. He overturned glasses and bottles, ordered a great fire to be kindled, and sent to the kitchen for a spit. "The

wretch!" he cried; "I will roast her, to teach her
better than to kill every thing in my palace."

The poor, trembling Medio Pollito was brought
before the fire, and the king already held her in
one hand and the spit in the other, when she
hastily murmured,

"River, river, come out of my throat, or I am a
little lost chicken!"

And behold! the river jumped out of her
throat, put out the fire, and drowned the king and
all the courtiers.

Medio Pollito, left mistress of the palace, sought
in vain for her hundred crowns; they had all
been spent, and no trace of them remained. But,
as there was no one on the throne, she mounted
it in the king's place, and the people welcomed
her accession with shouts of rejoicing; they were

delighted to have a queen that knew how to save.

This story appears somewhat extraordinary, and I should not tell it to you if it had not a moral, which seems, at first sight, to be, that it is not well to lend money to spendthrifts; but this is not the true one. The true moral of the story is, that we should always be obliging to every body, however absurd it may sometimes appear, for kindness never fails to be its own reward.

THE MAGIC AXE AND THE WHITE CAT.

AN honest wood-cutter once lived, with his wife and two children, Paul and Georgette, in a little cottage which he had built for himself in the midst of the forest. His wife was an active, good-natured woman, who kept every thing about her so neat that the humble cottage seemed fit for a rich man's dwelling. Georgette was just beginning to be able to help her mother. She washed the dishes after dinner, picked over the salad like a grown woman, and knew how to break the eggs nicely for an omelet. Paul went to the forest with his father, and amused himself by gathering strawberries, and making bouquets for his mother and sister while the wood-cutter was felling the great trees with his heavy axe; then, when they were on the ground, he chopped off the smaller branches with his little hatchet, and tied them up neatly in fagots. They all lived happy and contented, and there was not a family in the whole country that went to bed at night with a better conscience, thanking God for all his blessings.

Unhappily, at the close of a sultry summer, the whole country was ravaged by a terrible fever. The dead and dying were seen every where, and the humble cottage was attacked in turn by the scourge. The wife was the first to fall ill. As she was stretched helpless on the bed, languidly watching little Georgette trying to do her best, she was struck with terror to see her husband return from his work an hour earlier than usual, leaning, pale and trembling, on Paul's shoulder. The brave little boy had picked up the axe, which had fallen from his father's faltering hand, and thrown it across his other shoulder, though it almost crushed him with its weight. The wood-cutter lay down shivering by the side of his sick wife, and three days after the neighbors came to bear away his corpse.

When the poor woman saw her husband's body carried away, and felt herself alone with her children, her head distracted with grief and her limbs chained by sickness, she was seized with terror for her little ones, forgetting her own loss.

"What will become of you, my dear lambs," she cried, "now that you have lost your protector, and that I, wretched being, can do nothing for you?"

In her alarm, the tender mother was almost angry at herself for the sickness that rendered her helpless.

"Don't be afraid, mamma," exclaimed Paul, wiping away the tears that were flowing from his eyes. "I am a man now, and I know how to tie up fagots; I will support both of you."

And, stiffening his little arms, he tried to call to his aid the strength which he did not yet possess.

"And I," said Georgette, standing on tiptoe to reach the pillow, and kissing her mother tenderly, "I know how to keep house. Never mind your sickness, dear mamma; I will take care of every thing for you."

The sick woman smiled sadly, for she saw well that the poor little children could not do what they promised; but their courage and good-will filled her heart with a sweet consolation, which rested her from her suffering and sorrow. Worn out by the horrible nights that she had passed, she yielded to the influence of this instant of repose, and fell asleep peacefully under Georgette's kisses.

As soon as he saw his mother asleep, Paul took his hatchet, and went out on tiptoe, in haste to begin to play his part as the support of the family. He went straight to the tree which his father had just begun to cut down when the fever seized him, brandished his hatchet in the air, and set to work with ardor. His heart at first swelled with sorrow at the sight of the last notches made by his father's heavy axe, but another feeling soon took possession of him. It was in vain for him to strike; the hatchet, which served so admirably to cut off the slender boughs, made no impression on the great, knotty trunk. From time to time a little splinter flew in the air, but it was not missed; and Paul, already bathed in perspiration, felt himself discouraged to the bottom of his soul, without, however, abandoning his undertaking.

"No matter how long it takes, I shall cut it down at last," said he to himself.

Georgette, on her side, had undertaken the care of the house. The first glance around the room showed her the greatness of the task. Since her mother had kept her bed, every thing had been neglected. The furniture was covered with a thick layer of dust. She began by trying to wipe it off, and succeeded pretty well, although full half of the dust, which was lodged in the cracks and corners, escaped her duster; yet it was not bad for a beginning. She next thought of washing the dirty dishes that had accumulated during all this time in the bottom of the cupboard. Having no hot water, she brought from the brook that flowed before the door a bucket of pure fresh water, which took off the thickest of the dirt, and, by rubbing with the dish-cloth, she succeeded in washing the dishes tolerably clean. Up to this point every thing had gone well. But the thought suddenly struck her that Paul would come home from the forest at night and want his dinner. The poor little girl was in great perplexity, for she had never done any cooking. On no account would she have wakened her mamma, who was sleeping so sweetly. By rummaging the cupboard, she found there a piece of meat which her father had brought home on the fatal morning that he had been taken with the fever, and she resolved to make a soup of it, as she had often seen her mother do, without paying much attention, it is true, as is generally the case with children. It was easy enough to put the meat into a pot filled with water, and to hang the pot over the fire; but this done, poor Georgette stood before it with a blank look; she had come to the end of her knowledge.

Just at this moment the good fairies were holding council in a great golden cloud, from which they examined every thing that was taking place on earth, and sought out the wicked men who deserved punishment, and the good children who were in need of their aid. They saw Paul hacking away with all his might on the tree, and Georgette standing in contemplation before her dinner.

"Shall we leave these dear children in their trouble?" said the old fairy who presided over the assembly. "They have begun from the impulse of their heart; let us help them to finish."

Instantly two of the youngest fairies glided down the golden cloud, and poor Paul, whose strength was almost exhausted, suddenly saw a beautiful little dog standing before him — the smallest and most beautiful he had ever seen in his life. It was black, with long hair finer than silk, and a flame colored spot on the side of a slender nose of marvelous delicacy, which ended in a taper point, disclosing a double row of sharp teeth of dazzling whiteness. The dog frisked about Paul as if it wished to make friends with him, and raised its light and delicate fore paws, which resembled steel springs in the strength and suppleness of their movements. It reminded him of a little dog named Finette, which his father had formerly owned, and with which he had had many a game.

"You are very pretty, Finette," said he, with a sigh, "but you must let me work; I have no time to play with you."

"Oh! don't be afraid that I shall interrupt your work," said the dog; "on the contrary, I have come to help you."

"I shall not refuse any one's help; I am in

great need of it just now. See this great tree, which I am trying to cut down with my hatchet; it is not so easy as I thought."

"Well, we shall succeed, or my name is not Finette. But first throw me that useless tool, and look at the foot of the tree."

Paul looked on the ground before throwing away the hatchet, and stood wonder-struck at the sight of a great axe, which appeared heavier than his father's.

"Ah! dear Finette, what do you think that I can do with that axe? I can hardly raise it above my head."

"Try!" And the little dog sprang toward the

hatchet as if she would have snatched it from his hands.

Paul, who never shrank from fatigue, bravely picked up the axe, and, raising it with a great effort, let it fall on the tree. At the first stroke it swept away all the jagged notches which the hatchet had left in the upper part of the cleft as smoothly as a plane, and struck off a huge chip, which the little wood-cutter viewed with admiration. The second stroke was still better, and the courageous boy perceived, on redoubling his efforts, that they were less painful at each blow. The massive handle, which he had had great difficulty at first in grasping with both hands, continually shrunk in his fingers. The helve also became thinner, and seemed to him lighter and lighter, while at the same time the blade grew as keen as a razor. Never had axe cut so well. Finette gamboled round Paul, and every time her paw or tail touched him, he felt himself stronger, his blows were more vigorous and better aimed, and the chips fell like hail about him. In less than an hour the tree, cut almost completely through, bent backward with a terrific crash. Paul had just time to spring aside, when the giant, overthrown by the little hand which at first had seemed so inoffensive, fell heavily to the ground, crushing the bushes in its fall, and covering a vast space with its branches.

Finette barked, and instantly there appeared a little dwarf, no higher than a boot. He picked up the hatchet, and began to chop off the branches, with which he strewed the ground in the twinkling of an eye. No sooner was this done than a swarm of large ants came from the grass, and drew away the boughs, which piled themselves up of their own accord into bunches of fagots, while Paul, wonder-struck, took Finette in his arms, and danced about for joy.

"If this is all it costs, I will soon cut down another," cried he, as soon as he had taken breath. And again raising his beloved axe, which had become as keen and polished as a razor, he struck a second tree, still larger than the first, which it cut like butter.

In the mean time quite as extraordinary things had been taking place in the cottage. Poor Georgette crouched before the fire, and, not knowing what better to do, heaped log after log on it, for wood is always plenty at a wood-cutter's dwelling. The water was already making that peculiar hissing so well known to cooks, which comes from the kettle when it is about to boil, and Georgette was all eyes and ears, when a mew called her attention elsewhere, and a white head, with green eyes, rubbed against her hand. A great white cat, of wonderful beauty, had just entered without ceremony by an open window, and was stalking about the room as if perfectly at home.

Georgette stroked him on the forehead, the place where cats like to be scratched. "Ah! poor Imp," said she (Imp was the name of a kitten that she had loved dearly, and since it had disappeared she had called all the cats that she saw by that name), "ah! poor Imp, I am in great trouble."

"I have come to help you out of it," answered the cat, seating himself before her, and brushing his tail to the right and left.

"You help me out of it!" said Georgette, laughing; "and how would you set about it? I have to make soup for my brother Paul when he comes from the forest, and cats know nothing about cooking."

"I will show you how to make it, or my name is not Imp. In the first place, let us rake down this fire, which is enough to roast an ox. Soup needs to be boiled slowly."

Joining this action to his words, Imp lightly touched the great pile of fire-brands with his paw, when they instantly fell down, and buried themselves in the burning ashes, and a slow, gentle blaze rose from the embers.

"Let us see now whether you have forgotten

any thing." He delicately touched the water, which was beginning to simmer, with his paw, and licked the drops from the hair with his little red tongue.

"It seems to me that you have not thought of the salt."

Georgette blushed to the roots of her hair. She had indeed forgotten the salt.

When this grave omission had been remedied, the cat cast his eyes round the room. "It is not very badly swept," said he, "but it might be cleaner."

In an instant twelve little mice climbed on the furniture, each carrying in her front paw a square piece of flannel of the size of a carte de visite. They crept into all the corners, trotted along all the cracks, and rubbed so hard every where, that, when they had finished, the whole house seemed as bright as a new pin.

Georgette was delighted. "Ah! my dear Imp," said she, clasping the great white cat to her heart, "how grateful I am to you for having shown me so much. I will do the same to-morrow. It will please mamma."

As she spoke she glanced toward her mother, who was still sleeping soundly. In the excess of her joy she ran to kiss the hand that was lying on the coverlet, then returned to her pot, which

she had forgotten to watch while the mice were
cleaning the room. She shrank back in terror.
A grayish, dirty-looking scum covered the whole
surface of the pot.

"Imp, my dear Imp, come here quickly," she
cried, almost sobbing; "our soup is all dirty!"

Imp approached the fire and stood on his
hind paws.

"Don't be troubled," said he; "on the contrary,
it is cleansed. This must all be taken off carefully; it is the impurities of the salt and meat
which have risen to the surface."

And, pointing to a beautiful silver skimmer,
with an ebony handle, which had just hung itself

of its own accord on a nail at the corner of the fireplace, he showed her with a gesture how to use it.

When the pot was carefully skimmed, Imp took Georgette to the little garden which her father had planted behind the house, and made her pull up two fine carrots, a turnip, and four leeks, which, well washed and scraped, were tied together in a small bunch of parsley, and gently let down by the string into the pot, together with a head of Savoy cabbage, that danced on the top of the boiling water.

"Is this all?" asked Georgette.

"It needs but one thing more," answered the cat, as, jumping on her lap, he laid in it a small roasted onion. "Put this into the soup to color it, and then we will set the table and wait quietly for Paul."

In the mean time night was approaching. King Peter chanced that day to be hunting in the forest, which belonged to him, and where he kept every kind of game known, except, however, mischievous animals, for he would have been very sorry to have had any misfortune happen to one of his subjects on his account. He was the best-natured king that a people could desire; his only fault was that he was so fond of his crown that he always kept it on his head, even when he was hunting, and that he thought himself of a little different stuff from the rest of mankind; but he was so good that no one ever found fault with him for it.

This excellent king was in great perplexity for a quarter of an hour. Having suffered himself to be led away in pursuit of a hare by his great dog Phanor, he had lost sight of his attendants, who had followed another scent, and as princes are not obliged to know the roads, since they are always guided, he soon completely lost his way. He saw the sun rapidly sinking in the west with terror; not because he was afraid of spending the night in the woods, for he was a brave man; but among the prerogatives of his crown, the one to which he attached the most importance was the regularity of his meals, and the time for his dinner was fast approaching, without his seeing the way to reach home in time for it. Good-natured as he was, he stormed like a tempest, and scolded the impetuous Phanor, who, heedless of the august wrath, plunged headlong into the thickets, and cared more about finding the hare than the palace.

The sound of an axe in the silence of the forest led the wandering king to the place where Paul was just finishing cutting down his fourth tree. Phanor, who had ran on in advance, fell at once upon Finette, thinking to crush her with one blow of his great paw. He was soon punished, for Finette, springing in his face, struck him so hard with her paws that he fell back howling with pain. Paul, who had run to the aid of his little friend, stopped short when he saw the king among the trees, for it was very easy to recognize him by the crown on his head.

"Stop, my boy, not so fast!" cried the king. "That rascally dog is not worth much, but he is mine, and I will suffer no one to lay hands on him."

"Do not be angry with me, your majesty," answered Paul, respectfully. "I did not know that it was your dog, and I was defending mine."

"Well, well, my lad, we'll say no more about it. Where am I?"

"In the Great Thicket, a few steps from Osier Lake."

"That dog of a Phanor, he has led me in just the wrong direction! And what are you doing here, my little boy?"

"I am the son of your wood-cutter, who lived by the brook, and I am finishing my father's work."

"How is that? Has he gone away without saying any thing about it?"

"He died yesterday, sire."

And the child summoned up all his courage to keep back the large tears that filled his eyes.

"Poor little boy!" said the good king, with compassion. His crown preventing him from stooping to the child, he lifted him up and kissed him tenderly on both cheeks.

"Well," continued he, "who did all this work?"

A prodigious quantity of fagots was piled in heaps by the side of the gigantic trunks, and the ground was strewed with chips in all directions.

"I did it, sire, to-day. It is true that I had some help with the fagots."

"You, child! You are laughing at me."

"Oh, sire, it is not strange! I have such a good axe."

King Peter took a fancy to try this wonderful axe, with which a child had been able to do so much work in one day. It was one of the weaknesses of this worthy monarch to like to display his strength on every occasion. He was as broad-shouldered and athletic as a porter, and as his rivals were always careful to be beaten, he had cause to think himself one of the strongest men in the world; and, in his moments of boasting, he willingly compared himself to Charlemagne, who, it is said, lifted an armed knight from the ground with one hand. Fancying, therefore, that he was about to astonish Paul, and to fell the tree at one

blow, he seized the axe, which looked like a play·
thing in the child's hands. But no sooner had he
touched it than it resumed its size and weight,
and, as he was not in the habit of handling such
tools, the first blow that he struck with all his
might glanced off, the axe slipped from his hands,
and he came near falling backward on the ground.
His crown shook so much that, if he had not instantly raised his hand to it, it would have rolled
among the chips.

No other king would have ever forgiven Paul,
but King Peter was not a man to bear ill feeling
to any one. He was the first to laugh at his mis-
hap, but, for all that, he was vexed at it.

"Do you call that a good axe?" said he, a little
bitterly. "Do me the favor to go to work again.
I am curious to see it in your hands."

Paul gayly picked up the axe, which instantly
became small again, and, with four blows, finished
the tree, which bent, cracked, and made the whole
earth tremble with the weight of its fall.

The good king could not retain his admiration.
"My boy," cried he, "you can boast of not having
your equal. You shall go with me; I will take
you to my court."

The proposal took Paul by surprise. He turned to Finette as if to ask her advice. But fairy
animals never like to talk to children except when

they are alone with them. The little dog contented herself with wagging her tail against the
legs of the child, who found an answer at once.

"And you," said he, "would you not quit your
court to come and live with me?"

"That is a bad jest," answered the monarch,
frowning involuntarily. "In my court I am a
great king, and at your house I should be nothing but a great wood-chopper."

"And at your court," returned Paul, "I should
be nothing but a little wood-chopper, while here
I am a little king." As he spoke he sprang on
the largest of the fallen trees, and cast a triumphant glance over the scene of his exploits.

King Peter understood the jest, and remembered, at the same time, that it was past his hour for
dinner.

"You are a brave little boy; you always have
an answer ready for every thing," said he, in a
good-humored tone. "Take me to your house,
since you have spoken of it, and if any thing is
to be found to eat there, we will sit down to the
table together."

Rejoiced at so great an honor, Paul did not
wait for a second bidding. He shouldered his
axe, and they set out together at a rapid pace,
talking like two comrades. The handsome Phanor, who had scented out an air of superiority

in Finette, played the agreeable to her, court dog as he was, and was not afraid of compromising his station with a wood-chopper's dog.

Long before they reached the house a delicious smell of soup pleasantly tickled the nostrils of the good king, whose appetite had been sharpened by his walk.

"Ah! ah! my child," said he, "you seem to live well at your house. It was not a bad idea to invite myself to dinner."

Paul had been reflecting on the way with apprehension on the dinner that he might be able to offer his royal guest. What was his surprise, on entering the house, to find the table ready set with spotless linen, plates and glasses, which he no longer recognized, so bright had they grown, and a great tureen smoking with the savory soup which they had smelt so far off. His mother, sitting up in bed, with her hair combed and in a clean night-gown, had just finished sipping a cup of broth, which the cat had passed through a small piece of fine linen to strain off the grease, advising Georgette to weaken it with a little water.

The first outburst of joy passed, Paul threw himself in a chair, and began to weep bitterly.

"Why, what is the matter, dear brother?" said Georgette, running to him. "Are you not satisfied with the nice dinner I have prepared for you?"

"Oh yes, I am delighted; but I was thinking of poor papa, who would have enjoyed it so much with us."

"Come and kiss me, my child," said his mother from her bed. "You and your sister are good children; you make me very happy, and your father surely sees you from where he is."

And the three innocent beings, joining in a triple kiss, piously mingled their tears, which went to rejoice the dead in his new abode.

Hitherto no one had paid any attention to King Peter, and the good king was not offended at it; he was more disposed to weep than to be angry. When he thought that his hosts had sufficiently poured out their sorrow, he stepped forward.

"I share your grief, my good friends," said he, in a tone of emotion. Then, looking at the tureen with longing eyes, he added, "Will you permit me also to share your dinner?"

The mother uttered a cry of joyful surprise on seeing the king in her house, and Paul, stammering out his apologies, was about to ask for another plate, when he saw that it was already laid. Imp had called for it, and Georgette had obeyed without asking why.

There was nothing to be done, therefore, but to sit down to the table, and, while the two children related to each other the adventures of the day, King Peter, who listened to every thing, swallowed three large platesful of the best soup he had ever eaten in his life.

When he had finished he joined in the conversation, smacking his lips. "Since you are such favored children," said he, "I should like to be of the party. You and your cat, little girl, are the most famous cooks that I have ever met in my life. Come to my palace, and I will put you at the head of my kitchen."

To go to the king's palace was a very tempting thing to a little girl. "Can I take my mother and Paul with me?" asked Georgette, timidly.

The cat sprang on the bed, growling, and Finette pressed against Paul's legs.

"And your father, my child," cried her mother, sorrowfully, "could you also take him with you?"

"You must excuse us, sire," said Paul, with tears in his eyes, "but we have some one here who can no longer go with us, and who would be lonely should we leave him alone."

"Well, it shall not be said that I have done nothing for such worthy people. My little boy, you shall have the superintendence of all the wood-cutting in my forests; but try to moderate your axe a little, or they will soon be level with the ground from one end to the other."

Bread was thus secured for life to the humble family without taking them from the laborious life to which they were accustomed. Finette caressed the good king, who returned her caresses, and Imp sprang with one bound on his shoulder, and familiarly rubbed his whiskers against the royal mustaches.

At that instant the door opened, and the king's courtiers, who had been seeking him every where, uttered loud shouts of joy at his sight. They said afterward that a secret power, which they could not explain, had drawn them in that direction. King Peter went with them, with a contented heart and a satisfied stomach, carrying away the blessings of the whole family.

Finette and Imp went to sleep that night coiled up side by side in the chimney-corner, with their paws about each other. But the next morning they had disappeared. Paul and Georgette, on waking, saw in their place two young ladies of marvelous beauty, each with a key in her hand.

"Here," said they to the children, giving them the keys, "these are for your wedding-day. Continue to labor industriously, and to make your mother happy, and heaven will watch over you."

Saying this, they ascended again to the beautiful golden cloud, to relate to the other fairies the success of their mission.

The two children rushed to the door, and followed them with their eyes as far as they could see. When they looked again toward the ground, they saw, to their great astonishment, two beautiful little houses on each side of their mother's cottage. They tried their keys, which fitted exactly, and, having opened the doors, they entered the houses, and found them supplied with every thing that was needed for housekeeping. In Paul's there was a complete assortment of all the tools necessary for a woodman, and in Georgette's a set of copper kitchen utensils, which shone as brightly as if they had been made of gold.

They took up their abode in them on their wedding-day. Paul married the miller's daughter, the most promising and virtuous young girl in the whole country, and Georgette a young wood-cutter, the handsomest lad for ten leagues around, and as strong and good as their father had been. Both had lovely children, that were dandled every day on the knees of the old grandmother, and, when the latter went to rejoin her dear husband, she quitted life thanking heaven for the happiness it had given her. Paul lived to a

 Home Fairy Tales.

good old age, and was so much respected by his neighbors that he was chosen mayor of the town to which his cottage belonged—a high rank for a poor wood-cutter to attain.

PETER AND PAUL.

PETER was a small man; he was very, very small. He was well made, in spite of his short stature; he carried his head erect, and made the most of his inches; but it was all in vain for him to draw himself up; do what he might, he was still a little man.

His neighbor Paul was one of the largest men that was often seen; and, though they lived on very good terms, this mortifying contrast was a cause of unceasing vexation to little Peter. He never tired of throwing out sarcasms against those who were too tall; and, setting out from the principle, which none can dispute, that merit is not measured by size, he invariably drew the conclusion that small men were far superior to large ones.

Paul, who was as good as good could be, let him talk without losing his temper. He shrugged his shoulders a little at times, indeed; but this took place so far above the head of the orator that he never saw it. When they were walking together in the street, Paul even carried his condescension so far as to pretend to take Peter's arm, so as to seem to be leaning on him. He would let his arm fall the whole length, and pass his large hand under the shoulder of Peter, who crooked his elbow as well as he could.

One fine summer's day they took a walk in the country. As they were returning home, a little fatigued after rambling hither and thither, they suddenly found themselves before a little river which barred the way. They spied a bridge across it, indeed, but it was full a mile off. The water was clear and transparent, and, at first sight, on looking at the white pebbles and moss that covered the bottom, it did not seem more than four or five feet deep any where.

"This is capital!" cried Paul. "I feel exactly like taking a bath. I am going to wade across the stream." With these words he began to take off his clothes and make a package of them, which he took in his hand.

"Don't you wish me take you on my back, my friend?" said he to Peter.

"It seems to me that I have legs as well as you, and am quite able to walk," answered Peter, angrily.

"Then you had better go up to the bridge yonder," said Paul; "I will wait for you on the other side."

Peter was furious. "Does this great Goliath pretend to humiliate me?" muttered he, between his teeth. "I will show him that I am as good as he. Where one man can go, another can go likewise." Saying this, he took off his clothes in turn, and bravely entered the river, his package in his hand. Scarcely had he taken a step when he found himself up to his chin in the water. By holding his clothes above his head, he managed to keep them dry; but, happening to stumble, he involuntarily lowered his arm, when lo! the precious package was wet through and through. In an instant the water became deeper, he lost his footing, and the current was bearing him away, when Paul, who was watching him from the shore, strode through the water with his long legs, and, stretching out his great hand, seized the imprudent Peter, and brought him safe and sound to land.

Peter was obliged to wait more than an hour for his clothes to dry, and while they were drying he had full time for reflection. "Little folks are as good as large folks," said he at last, when he was dressed, "that I will maintain to my dying breath; but they can not do the same things."

THE ENCHANTED WATCH.

Once upon a time there was a young girl who never knew what time it was. I can not tell you whether she thought much about it, neither can I tell you how often she grieved her father, who had no child but her, and who consequently spoiled her, by making him miss his appointments, or how often the coach had to wait for whole hours before the door when she was about to make a journey. There were no railroads in those days, fortunately for her, for she would always have been obliged to go in the next day's train. One day an impatient coachman christened her Miss Tardy, and the name henceforward clung to her. When she had taken her time, turned round a hundred times, conversed at her leisure with the mirror, and opened and shut the door half a score of times to see whether she had not forgotten something, she came in hurriedly, apologizing in a pretty childish way for being late, accusing herself of giddiness, and touchingly deploring her short memory. The truth was, that Fanny, for that was her name, thought a great deal of her own comfort, and very little of that of others.

Her old godmother, who saw her from time to time, wrote to her one day that she was coming to dine with her at noon. People dined at noon in those days. She was a fairy celebrated for her exactness; this had procured her the name of the fairy Punctuality, of which she was very proud. It was of no use to talk to her of fifteen minutes' grace; to her noon was not five minutes before noon, or five minutes after noon, but noon. At the first stroke of twelve she set foot on the first step of the staircase, and entered the dining-room as the last stroke was sounding.

The table was set—that was the work of the servants — but Fanny was still promenading about the city. She had suddenly recollected that she had long owed a visit to an intimate friend, and as people were much earlier risers at that time than now, it appeared very natural to make calls five or six hours after sunrise. Her friend had just received a whole assortment of dresses and bonnets in the latest fashion, and Miss Tardy came in time to witness the unpacking. It was necessary instantly to try on all these beautiful things, and to compare them, criticise them, and devise improvements of the highest importance. The conversation became so in-

teresting that the poor godmother was as completely forgotten as though she had never existed.   At last, about one o'clock, Fanny's stomach admonished her that she had not yet dined,
and the thought of her godmother naturally re-
curred to her memory after that of dinner. She
hastily took leave, but on the way home she saw
so many fine things in the shop windows that a
full quarter of an hour was taken up in looking
at them, and even then the time seemed short to
her.

On reaching her door Fanny heard that her
godmother had been waiting a long time. Unfortunately, her shoes hurt her. She had put on a
tight pair that morning, in order to be equal with
her friend, who had a small foot. She could not
reasonably be expected to sit down to the table
with an instrument of torture on her limbs. She
went softly to her room, therefore, where she lux-
uriously buried her bruised feet in a charming
little pair of furred slippers. But the rest of
her dress no longer matched with the slippers.
It would have been wanting in respect to her
godmother not to make every thing correspond;
besides, somebody might come in, and it would
have been necessary to enter into tiresome explanations. All this took so much time, that it was
past two o'clock when Fanny went down to the

parlor in a bewitching pink and white morning-dress, which fitted her to perfection.

The good godmother was asleep in one of those great easy-chairs which are no longer in fashion, and I even believe that she was snoring a little. She awakened as the door opened hastily.

"Oh, godmother, I am so ashamed and sorry! Was ever any body so thoughtless as I?"

"No matter, my child," said the good lady, who was always indulgent to others; "I have slept a little while waiting for you, and it has done me no harm. What time is it?"

"Oh, pray don't ask me; you will make me die of shame!"

And she threw herself before the clock with a childish air; but the old fairy, whose eyesight was still good, frowned a little as she saw that the hour-hand was past two.

The dinner was not very nice, as may well be imagined; but the fairy, who really loved her goddaughter, took every thing in good part, and jested so pleasantly on the burned meat and turned creams, that the mistress of the house, speedily reconciled with herself, was greatly diverted.

The time passed quickly, and it was already four o'clock, when Fanny's father entered in great haste. He had driven from the country at full gallop, and had nearly broken his carriage, to avoid being late.

" Well, Fanny, are you ready?" he cried, as soon as he opened the door. He stood still in amazement on seeing Fanny, negligently stretched in an easy-chair, in her pink and white wrapper, with her feet to the fire, slowly sipping her coffee.

" What!" he exclaimed, "did you not receive my letter of yesterday morning?"

" Your letter, dear papa? Yes, I received it; but don't you see that my godmother is here?"

" Excuse me, madam," said the angry father, bowing. "Forgive my abruptness; but this child will kill me with vexation."

" Why, what has the dear child done?"

" Judge for yourself. I wrote to her yesterday that I should come to-day to take her to visit Prince Pandolph, who has invited us to his villa. I told her to be ready at four o'clock, and that we should not have a minute to lose, for he was to take us in his own carriage, and we could not think of making him wait. It was my only opportunity of talking with him alone about my great enterprise, the success of which none but he can insure; and here it is lost!"

" Well, papa, why can't you go without me?"

" You know very well, unhappy child, that it is you that is invited, and not I. It is your beautiful voice that is wanted for the evening's entertainment. If I appear without you the prince will frown on me, and good-by to my figures! Your fine morning-dress has made me lose more than a hundred thousand ducats."

"Come, be calm, my dear sir," said the fairy, who saw her goddaughter change countenance (a hundred thousand ducats is no trifle). "It was in my company that the dear child forgot you; it belongs to me to repair the evil."

Saying this, she passed her hand over the unlucky morning-dress, which was instantly transformed into an enchanting evening costume, as fine as could be desired for a visit to a prince's villa.

Fanny, who was naturally beautiful, shone like a star in this brilliant dress, which lacked but one thing—the ornament which ladies are in the habit of wearing in their belt.

"Wait a moment," said the fairy to the impatient father, who was dragging away his daughter; "let me finish my work." And she threw over her goddaughter's neck a magnificent gold chain, at the end of which hung a love of a little watch, of enameled gold set with great pearls.

"Here, puss," said she, kissing her spoiled child on the forehead, "here is something to aid your bad memory. With this you can be sure of never again forgetting the time."

You must know that watches were invented by the fairy Punctuality in her youth, but none are for sale now in the shops like those which were made in the beginning. Fanny's watch had the magic virtue of warning its wearer of the hour appointed, and of giving her no rest till she had set about doing what she had agreed to do. If watch-making had not so much degenerated in our days, what a fine New Year's gift would such a watch be to ladies!

Prince Pandolph was a good old prince, who was passionately fond of music, and who had heard the highest praises of Fanny's voice. He was full of attention to her, and of affability to her father, who adroitly took advantage of the freedom of conversation in the carriage to make the first overtures with respect to his famous enterprise. A great number of guests were found assembled at the villa, which was situated amid the most beautiful gardens that ever were seen. After the dinner, which was long and sumptuous, the ladies expressed a wish to see the gardens, and the company dispersed among the avenues and groves.

"Above all, my friends," said the prince, on seeing them go—"above all, do not forget that our entertainment begins at nine o'clock."

And as Fanny passed before him on her father's arm, he stepped toward her and whispered in her ear, "You know that you are to open it; do not fail to be in time."

As I have just told you, the gardens were magnificent. The most beautiful trees were collected there from the four quarters of the globe, and running brooks flowed capriciously in all directions along the footpaths, or spread in limpid sheets in the midst of the broad green lawns, while the moon shone in the heavens, and rendered all these marvels still more fascinating.

The group of which the father and daughter made a part had taken refuge in a verdant nook on the shore of a little lake. Surrounded with a grove of dark firs, and silvered over by the rays of the full moon, it looked like an ebony cup full of silver. Seated in rustic chairs, they abandoned themselves peacefully to that mute contemplation of the beauties of nature so particularly agreeable to those who have dined well.

Suddenly a sound was heard: Tick, tick, tick, tick!

"It is nine o'clock," cried Miss Tardy, and, quickly rising, she took the way to the villa, followed by all the guests.

"What a good little watch my godmother has given me!" she exclaimed with delight to her father.

The beautiful Fanny had received from heaven an enchanting voice, flexible, fresh, full, and silvery in tone, which went straight to the soul, and she governed it with so much taste that none could have doubted that she felt what fell from her lips. On this evening she enjoyed a real triumph. Prince Pandolph was enthusiastic in his delight, and her father, having met him at a happy moment on the threshold of his study, persuaded him to sign on the spot the contract which he had vainly solicited for a year from the ministers. The enterprise in question was one as advantageous to the state as to the contractor, but which had nevertheless been slumbering for years in the official bureaux. What the reasoning of the most important men had been unable to obtain, a beautiful voice obtained without reasoning. So goes the world!

It was late at night when they returned to town. The father knew not how to express his gratitude to his daughter.

"To-morrow morning," said he, "I will take you to Mr. Jacobus's" (this was the fashionable jeweler of the city), "and clasp myself on this pretty little arm the antique cameo bracelet that you asked me for the other day. At what time will you go? will ten o'clock be too soon?"

"Oh no, let us go at nine. I have been dying to have the bracelet ever since I saw it. How it will spite the counselor's daughter, who has one of almost exactly the same style, but not half so handsome!"

"Nine o'clock be it, then. And what will you do all the morning?"

"I will tell Jenny, when I get home, to send for the dress-maker at ten precisely; I must have some new dresses."

"Get whatever you like, my dear little nightingale. The plumage must correspond with the song. And, if it suits you, we will breakfast at eleven. I have a crowd of people to see to-morrow, in order to set my enterprise going."

"Eleven o'clock be it, dear papa. But don't forget to return in time to take me to the baron's ball; he was so anxious that we should be there."

"Don't be alarmed; on no account would I keep such a jewel of a child waiting."

And petting, caressing, and complimenting each other in this manner, they reached home, where they slept a golden sleep, such as is given by a hundred thousand ducats.

The next morning, at nine, Fanny was no longer sleeping, but she was enjoying that dozing state so pleasant to the indolent, and far more delightful than real sleep, because you feel yourself sleeping, and enjoy the bed with the knowledge that you are there.

Tick, tick, tick, tick!

"Ah! I know; it is time to go for the bracelet. A little patience; only five minutes more!"

Tick, tick, tick, tick!

"Well, well, you little noisy thing, I will obey. To tell the truth, I am in somewhat of a hurry to see the bracelet on my arm."

She rose with a tolerably good grace, dressed more quickly than usual, and before half past nine entered the shop of Mr. Jacobus, leaning on the arm of her father, who was even more amiable than the evening before. He had been dreaming all night of his triumph.

The bracelet was soon bought; but the jeweler, who knew his trade, opened, as if by chance, some beautiful jewel-boxes which were at hand. There were strings of pearls interspersed with large rubies, which produced a marvelous effect, sets of sapphires set in silver, which would have excited the envy of a princess, and necklaces of diamonds, almost as sparkling as drops of dew. Fanny's eyes lighted up, and, as her father smiled approvingly, she soon entered into an animated conversation with Jacobus, which had ended in nothing serious, when the hand of the great clock at the bottom of the shop reached ten.

Tick, tick, tick, tick!

"Thank you for your advice, my dear, but the dress-maker can wait," said Fanny.

Tick, tick, tick, tick!

She took off the watch and handed it to her father. "Please put it in your pocket," said she; "it is too annoying."

Her father took the watch and, seeing a friend passing in the street, he went to the door to speak to him.

Ting, ting, ting, ting!

The watch raised its voice, forced as it was to make itself heard at a greater distance. The people in the shop turned round to see where the noise came from. It was necessary to cut short the negotiation, and the dress-maker was saved waiting an indefinite time; but, innocent as she was, she had to take the blame, for the compliments that Fanny paid her in her own mind on leaving the shop were any thing but flattering.

No sooner, however, had the dress-maker displayed her stuffs and showed her patterns, than all the ill humor disappeared. A dress of gray silk, trimmed with point lace, was the first agreed upon; then a cloak of garnet velvet, embroidered with gold; then, a morning-dress of India muslin that might have been passed through a child's ring. Fanny was about to look at something else, when a glance at the clock warned her that breakfast-time was approaching.

"This provoking watch will disturb me again," thought she; and, going into the next room under some pretext, she hid her godmother's gift in the bottom of a wardrobe.

But scarcely had she time to enter into a new negotiation when the dress-maker turned her head.

Ding dong, ding dong!

"Oh, Miss Fanny! what noise is that? Some one is trying to burst the wardrobe open."

"It is nothing; let us go on."

Ding dong, ding dong!

"There is surely some one there. Can it be that a robber has entered the house?"

"It is nothing, I tell you; unroll this cambric."

Ding dong, ding dong!

The watch sounded louder and louder, and the dress-maker, half dead with fright, was unable to pay the least attention to what was said to her.

Fanny was forced to send her away, and to go to the dining-room, where her father, in haste to attend to his business, was impatiently pacing the room.

"Oh, it is very good of you, dear Fanny, to be so punctual.   My time is precious to-day."

And, tenderly embracing her, he led her to her place, where the sight of a good breakfast and the attentions of her father soon made her forget her last vexation.

As they were beginning their breakfast a servant entered to say that old Valentine wished to know whether he could speak to Miss Fanny. This was an unfortunate old man whom she had taken under her protection, as young ladies are apt to do.   She had heard of him one day when she happened to be in a benevolent mood, and had undertaken to look after him, without really knowing what she intended to do for him.   From time to time, when too closely pressed by want, he presented himself at her house, and never went away, it must be confessed, empty handed.   This time he came at an unlucky moment, for Fanny's father had no time to lose, and did not wish the breakfast interrupted.

"Tell him to come back at two o'clock," said Fanny, resolving in her heart to be generous, in view of the good fortune of the night before.

Unhappily, on going to her room, she found a new book which the bookseller had just sent her. It was a novel by one of the most fashionable authors, and the subject was as exciting as possible. The story was of a young woman, as beautiful as an angel, who thought herself justified in committing every kind of crime because her husband was not perfect. To cut the first pages, and throw herself into an easy-chair, the precious book in hand, was the work of an instant. The plot became more and more exciting, and she was approaching the crisis that was to decide the fate of the interesting heroine, when, on looking at her watch, she saw that it was a quarter before two.

She rang instantly for Jenny. "That tiresome Valentine will soon be here, with his endless stories," said she. "Tell him that I am not at home." Then, the fatal watch recurring to her mind, "Stop! take this watch," said she, "and put it in the cellar, so that I may be rid of it."

She eagerly resumed the reading of the moving pages, so full of useful lessons.

The clock was about to strike two when old Valentine appeared for the second time. The poor man had had nothing to eat for two days, and his heart swelled with grief on hearing that Fanny was not at home. He wiped away a tear, and was already taking his leave with a humble bow, when every one in the house started.

Bang, bang, bang, bang!

And sounds like pistol-shots fired in rapid succession came from the cellar. The neighbors began to scream, thinking that the people in the house were shooting each other.

Jenny ran to her mistress, who had thrown down her book. "Do you hear that, Miss Fanny?"

Bang, bang, bang, bang!

"Yes, I hear it. I am sure that the watch is at its old tricks again. A fine gift my godmother has made me!"

Bang, bang, bang, bang!

"Well, well, I am coming."

She rose to receive her protégé, and all became silent. I must say to her praise that poor old Valentine was not the sufferer from the violence done to his protectress. No sooner did she see him, with his eyes moist with tears and his cheeks hollow with hunger, than she was touched with compassion, for her heart was good at the bottom. She welcomed him with her most gracious smile, ordered dinner to be brought him, listened to him, comforted him, sent him away with a well-filled purse, and returned to her room with a light heart, happier assuredly than if she had had leisure to finish her book.

"Bring me the watch," said she to Jenny, "and help me to dress, for I must think of getting ready for the ball if I would not be rung up again."

The preparations lasted long, as you may believe. At last all was finished, and she was about to set out, when a lumbering carryall rattled over the pavement and stopped at the door, and an old peasant woman alighted, who asked in a loud tone for her child, her dear little Fanny, whom she wished to see once more before she died. It was her old nurse, who had been called by some unexpected business to the city, and who was obliged to return the next day to her village, many leagues distant. Such an opportunity was not likely to occur again in her life; and when she learned that her dear Fanny was going to the ball, she began to cry and bewail her ill luck.

Fanny had always kept a pleasant memory of her nurse, whom she had often seen again in her childhood. She clasped her tenderly in her arms, at the risk of rumpling her dress, which is not a slight mark of affection in a lady. Seeing that nothing could calm her grief, she promised her solemnly only to remain a little while at the ball, and to return before the evening was over; and at that moment she really intended to do so, for the old woman's grief pained her. On this promise the nurse became calm. She was seated on a sofa, with a nice little dinner before her; the

coachman cracked his whip, and off went Fanny
and her father to the ball.

The motion of the carriage and the coolness of
the night air somewhat chilled her first emotion
on the way. The ball was the last of the season,
and the counselor's daughter was to be there
with the bracelet which she was so anxious to
eclipse. Her dress, though slightly rumpled,
could have few rivals, and it would really be a
pity to have taken so much pains for ten minutes'
triumph. On reflection, she resolved that the
evening should be given to the ball, but that she
would return home precisely at midnight.

No sooner had she made this arrangement than
a terrible thought struck her; it was not exactly
what she had promised, and what if the watch
should disapprove of it? What a scandal would
it make in this brilliant assembly, where all the
illustrious personages of the court and town were
expected! A word to the coachman, and the
horses turned toward the wall; then her tiny
hand, which had been playing with her belt, gently unfastened the watch and threw it over the
wall into the ditch.

"I am rid of it at last," said she, with a sigh of
relief.

Fanny's entrance made a sensation. Her dress
was beautiful, and she wore in her hair a spray of

verbena, with a stem of gold, leaves of malachite, and flowers of amethyst, which excited general admiration. It was a little heavy, but she did not feel it. The counselor's daughter saw the bracelet, and turned pale under her rouge—a triumph well worth the embraces of all the nurses in the world.

Nevertheless, the joy of the beautiful dance was not at first untroubled. It seemed to her at times that she heard strange sounds rumbling through the air, which smothered the notes of the band, and made her lose the measure, and which might be the last moans of the unfortunate friend that she had cast away. But the excitement of the ball soon rose to her brain, and all was forgotten. Midnight found her flushed and breathless, her waist encircled by the arm of the most brilliant waltzer in the room, a handsome young colonel, with a beautiful waxed mustache, and a coquettish scar which he had brought back from the war, and which became him wonderfully.

Boom, boom, boom, boom!

The band stopped short. The peals of thunder, for no other term of comparison could be found for the noise, succeeded each other without interruption, and the whole town was roused in an instant. The good women began to cry that the end of the world had come. The unhappy Fanny instantly understood what was the matter, and, in her fright, lost her presence of mind. Instead of quietly returning home, which would have put a stop to all this horrible uproar, she rushed into the street, wild with terror, and ran at full speed toward the place whence the noise came. The streets were deserted, but the houses were already illuminated, and the windows were filled with terror-struck people, in all possible costumes, timidly looking out into the darkness to try to discover what had happened, while the boom, boom, boom, still continued, increasing in force at each peal.

The young girl, running alone in the street in a ball dress, attracted all eyes, and every one asked who she could be. She fell among a company of firemen, who were making their rounds with their torches to see if something was not on fire, and the wag of the company, putting his light to her face, exclaimed, laughing, " It is Miss Tardy; she has lost the time, and is running to find it."

She reached the gate out of breath, and had great difficulty in gaining admission. Once inside the wall, she ran to the ditch in search of the watch. She did not have to look long, for the thunder-claps guided her more surely than any light could have done. Just as she had seized the terrible watch, and, in her rage, was preparing to dash it against the stone wall, she felt a hand on her arm. She turned and saw her godmother, who said, in a tone of gentle reproach,

"What are you trying to do, my child? You will never succeed."

She took the watch, which instantly became silent, and hung it again around the neck of her goddaughter, who trembled with shame and repentance.

"Neither violence nor stratagem can prevail against my gifts," said she. "The only thing to be done is to obey, and you will always find this your wisest course."

In an instant Fanny found herself transported to her own room, grasping the hands of her old nurse, who wept with tenderness, and who appeared to her a hundred times more charming than the handsome colonel.

I need not say that this was her last attempt to rebel against the tyrannical protector which she wore at her belt, and which more than once procured for her the sweetest joys by forcing her to sacrifice her fancies to her duties.

If there are any children here who have likewise received from their godmothers those little watches which go tick, tick, when they forget their duty, I advise them always to bear in mind the story of Miss Tardy. To try to hide our faults from ourselves is the best means of drawing every one's attention to them; and the surer the hiding-place appears, the greater is their noise.

POVERETTA.

THERE was once a rich nobleman who died, leaving two daughters. According to the custom of the country, he bequeathed all his property to the elder, that she might the better support the honor of the family—that is to say, keep fine carriages and a host of servants, wear costly dresses, marry a fortune, and so forth. Her mother had died long before, and the good nobleman with his last breath entreated the heiress to take good care of her sister, who would have no other support than herself.

The elder sister was named Barbara. She was a tall and beautiful girl, with a dazzling complexion, luxuriant black tresses, and magnificent teeth, but proud and selfish, thinking of nothing but shining in society and taking her pleasure.

The younger, on the contrary, was a little, delicate girl, pale and puny, and almost ugly, except her eyes, which were very beautiful; and so feeble and slender in body that she had been called Poveretta, an inglorious name, with which she was perfectly content. Indeed, she was the best and gentlest child that could have been seen, jealous of no one, always happy in the happiness of others, and forgetful of herself when others did not think of her.

From the beginning, Barbara, as might have been expected, entirely forgot the request of her father. Wholly engrossed in her new fortune, she looked on Poveretta only as an upper servant, lodged her in a little chamber under the roof, and would not even permit her to sit with herself at the table, where the choicest dishes were served up to Barbara, while her sister lived meagerly on whatever the servants chose to bring her.

Poveretta made no complaint, and loved her sister none the less. She strove to obey all her wishes, not through submission, but through real pleasure, for the idea of pleasing her was sufficient to delight her heart. From morning to night she was on her feet, executing or anticipating Barbara's orders; but, in spite of her threadbare clothes, no one would have mistaken her for any other than one of the family, so much did her bright, happy face, and the quiet assurance of her manners, show that she felt at home under the inhospitable roof of her haughty sister.

Things had gone on in this way for a long time, when one day Barbara was invited, with her sister, to a ball, which was to be given in the king's palace. It was her first ball since her father's death, and you may judge what an event it was to her. From the moment that the precious invitation arrived nothing else was talked of in the house. The footmen scoured the city, the most skillful hair-dressers and dress-makers were sent for, and the great sitting-room on the first floor was turned into an immense workshop, under the eye of the beautiful Barbara, who went from one to another trying on, criticising, studying the probable effect of all the marvels that were begun, and enjoying in advance her coming triumph. It is needless to say that poor Poveretta was not thought of; Barbara did not even remember that her sister had been invited, and Poveretta herself had forgotten it. As none of the seamstresses could compare with her in skill and taste, she naturally took the lead, and clapped her hands like a child when she succeeded in pleasing her sister.

The night before the ball Poveretta's godmother returned from a long journey to fairy-land, where she had had many things to set in order, for she was a fairy herself, and one of the most respected among her sisters. As she was very fond of her goddaughter, who was indebted to her in great part for her lovely character, her first thought was to visit Poveretta as soon as she heard of her father's death. She entered her carriage, drawn

I

by four milk-white deer swifter than the wind,
and drove like lightning into the court-yard, the
gates of which had been left wide open to make
way for a fine new coach ordered for the occasion,
which the carriage-maker himself had brought
with great ceremony. Without stopping to make
inquiries of the servants, for she was well acquainted with the house, she went straight up stairs,
where she found Miss Barbara stretched on a sofa,
resting from her fatigue, for she had just tried on
six magnificent dresses, each more beautiful than
the other, without being able to decide which to
wear.

When the fairy asked to see Poveretta, Barbara, who did not feel quite at ease before her,
and who dreaded the interview, tried to stammer
out some excuse.

"She is very busy just now," said she, "but if
you could call again—"

"Send for her; I wish to see her," interrupted
the fairy with so commanding an air that Barbara
instantly obeyed, though much against her will.

Poveretta, on hearing that her godmother was
there, rushed from the hall without stopping to
shake off the threads that clung to her dress,
and darted like lightning to her sister's room,
where she threw herself weeping into the arms
of the fairy.

"What a strange dress you have on, my child!" said her godmother, looking from one sister to the other. "And where did all these threads come from?"

"I have on my every-day clothes," replied Poveretta, innocently, "and I am just now very busy at sewing. We are making a dress for my sister to wear to-morrow to the king's ball. You will see how beautiful she will be, my dear godmother."

"Is it possible that your sister is not invited?" asked the fairy, turning toward Barbara.

"Yes, she is invited; but what would she do in such a place?"

"I mean that she shall go, at any rate; and as it is not proper that you should go alone to such a great assembly, I will come to-morrow for you both."

Poveretta burst into a fit of laughter. "Why, godmamma," said she, "I have nothing that looks like a ball-dress. How can I appear at the palace by the side of my sister, who will shine like a star?"

"Don't trouble yourself about that," returned Barbara, trying to conceal her vexation; "I can lend you one of my old dresses, and you can alter it to fit you after you have finished my dress."

"Oh, how good you are! I shall be so glad to see how much you are admired."

The fairy kept silence. After a moment's reflection she turned to her goddaughter. "Take me to your room, my child," she said, in a softened voice. "I wish to be alone with you."

"There is no need of that," interrupted Barbara, blushing in spite of herself. "Stay here; I will leave you alone."

"No, I thank you. But, as I intend to stay here for some hours, you will oblige me by inviting me to dinner."

Saying this, she went out with Poveretta, who clung to her, kissing her hands, so delighted was she to see her.

You may think that the godmother took a great deal upon herself; but you must know that, during the father's lifetime, she had always possessed great authority in the house, and that the haughty Barbara had been accustomed from infancy to obey her.

"How tiresome!" cried the latter, when she was alone. "I can't help having Poveretta to dinner, and every thing must be turned topsy-turvy in the dining-room." And, without thinking of resistance, she went to give the necessary orders.

In the mean time Poveretta led her godmother up one flight of stairs after another. Having at last reached her room, she joyfully opened the door, and stood aside to make room for the fairy,

who paused, seized with indignation, on the
threshold.

A paltry little pine couch, with a wretched
mattress and blanket, was the only piece of furniture of importance in the chamber, which had
been stripped when Poveretta was banished to it.
It must be said that Barbara had never seen the
room; it was a trifle of too little consequence to
call for her attention. A bit of carpet, full of
holes, and frayed at the edges, was stretched before the foot of the bed. A little rickety table
served at once as toilet-stand, dining-table, and
bureau, and the only chair in the room was beginning to lose its rushes. There were no curtains to the windows, and the walls were bare;
yet with all this there was an air of simple neatness, which gave a sort of charm to the wretched
lodging.

The fairy wiped away a tear that rolled down
her cheek, a bad sign for Barbara. If the tears
of fairies are rare, as every one knows, it is all the
more terrible for those who cause them to flow.

"How do you like this room, my dear child?"
said she at last, entering with an effort.

"Oh, very much, godmamma; there is such
a fine view here. Come and look out of the window."

Indeed, from this height the eye surveyed the

whole city, and discerned in the distance the country with its wind-mills, its clumps of trees, and its scattered cottages. Those who have always lived in the fields know not what happiness it is for the dweller in cities to see from his window a bit of landscape over the roofs of the houses.

The fairy, who had traveled too much to be so easily struck with admiration, soon left the window. She seated herself on the only chair in the room, took her goddaughter on her lap, and entered into a long conversation, interrupted from time to time by their mutual caresses.

The hour for dinner having come, the fairy was greatly astonished to see an immense table set for three, with the seats so far apart that they could scarcely hear each other. It was the table used for dinners of ceremony, outside of which Barbara received no guests; for, like a true egotist, she liked to dine alone, in order to keep all the choice tit-bits for herself. For this reason, in order to be perfectly at her ease, she had had a beautiful little table made for her own use, in the form of a semicircle, with her chair fitting in the middle, so that she had every thing ready at hand on each side of her.

"Do you usually dine at this great table?" asked the fairy of Barbara.

"Oh no, madam, this is set on your account. There is my table." And she pointed to the semicircular table, which the fairy eyed harshly.

"But where do you put Poveretta?"

"Oh, godmamma, I dine in my own room; it is more convenient for us both." The good girl said this in order to excuse her sister, for she had often sighed for those sweet hours of intimacy which are passed at the common table, and, indulgent as she was, she felt at the bottom of her heart that it was wrong in Barbara to refuse them to her.

The fairy said no more, and the dinner went on gloomily. When it was over Poveretta's godmother took her hand and Barbara's, and joined them with an air of authority.

"Two sisters should enjoy and suffer good and evil together. Let it never more be forgotten in this house!"

With these words she went out majestically, without looking behind her.

The sisters gazed at each other, with their hands still joined together. It was so long since Poveretta had touched her sister's hand that her little heart was ready to burst with joy. Looking at Barbara with eyes full of admiration, she threw her arms round her neck. "How beautiful you are to-day!" she exclaimed, lovingly.

Her godmother had found nothing to change in her; but she had redoubled by a magic spell the happiness already given her by her love for her sister.

A wholly different spell was cast on Barbara. The fairy had been too angry with her to make her a gift of love; she had only condemned her to share her sister's sufferings, whatever they might be, without working any change in her wicked feelings.

"How pale and puny you are!" said she, harshly, pushing Poveretta from her. She felt herself a prey to anguish, as if her own beauty had been suddenly taken from her. Wholly occupied hitherto in admiring herself, she had never thought of asking whether her sister was ugly or handsome; but now her pitiful aspect hurt her so much that she forgot her own advantages. Troubled more than we can tell at a feeling so new to her, she replied to the tender glances of the dear child by a look at once full of hate and terror. Poveretta, who had always been indifferent to her, suddenly became odious in her sight. Her sleeping heart was aroused to hate, and to hate is to suffer.

They went together to the work-room, but all Barbara's pleasure in the preparations was gone. Whether she examined a trimming or looked at a skirt, her eyes involuntarily turned to the fragile girl who was bending over her work, and trying to make up the lost time by greater activity. This spectacle was intolerable torture to the selfish Barbara, suddenly stripped of her armor of indifference. Unable longer to endure it, she rose suddenly and went to her room, and soon returned with an old dress of the last year's fashion, which she flung at her sister, saying, "There is something for to-morrow! Go to your room and arrange it; somebody else can do your work." From that moment she was able to contemplate at her ease the fine dresses which awaited her choice.

Love is blind, and that of Poveretta had been too much increased by the fairy for her to notice the contemptuous tone of her sister. She took the dress gratefully, gathered up a few bits of ribbon, scraps of lace, and cast-off flowers, and flew to her room, as light-hearted as a bird, to commence her work. Under her skillful fingers all the rubbish was transformed as if by enchantment. The dress, turned, mended, altered, and set off with a scrap of lace, might have been taken for new when it quitted her hands. It was already very late, but the industrious worker found time to devise a head-dress of enchanting grace and beauty—one of those articles made, as they say, out of nothing, but which surpass all the inventions of wealth when worn with style and elegance. Her dress finished, the idea of trying it on did not once occur to her, perhaps because she was too tired, and she fell asleep, thinking with delight that her sister would undoubtedly be queen of the ball.

The next evening, when the godmother came for the two sisters, Poveretta came from her own room looking like a little fairy. There was something enchantingly airy and exquisite in her whole appearance, and Barbara looked like an overdressed doll by her side. Through trying on and comparing the ornaments and embellishments, without knowing which to sacrifice, she had put on so many that they glittered gaudily, and called to mind a shop-window. Poveretta, whose taste was so fine, would certainly have thought this dress ridiculous on any one else; but, blinded by her love for her sister, she fell into ecstasies over it, and almost wept with delight and admiration.

"Oh, godmamma," she exclaimed, "how happy I am to see her so beautiful!" And her radiant face shone with such lustre that all the beauty of Barbara paled in comparison.

The latter, on the contrary, saw nothing of the grace and elegance which set off her sister's costume. Her imagination instantly brought before her eyes the sweepings of which it was composed; and, do what she might, the old dress, the bits of ribbon, the scraps of lace, and the cast-off flowers constantly appeared before her eyes. She lost sight of her own magnificence, and entered the ball-room with a contracted brow and gloomy expression, which took away all pleasure in looking at her.

The result of this was that all the homage and attentions were lavished on Poveretta, and that no one paid any attention to Barbara, a just punishment for her pride and harshness.

There was a young prince at the king's court who was as witty and good as he was brave and handsome. In spite of his youth, he was already celebrated for many heroic deeds in battle, and all the mothers who had marriageable daughters paid court to him. His family living on an estate near their country seat, he had been a friend of the two sisters from childhood, and they had often played together at hide-and-seek, and blindman's-buff. A marriage between him and Barbara had even been talked of during her father's lifetime, and she had almost accustomed herself, without really knowing why, to look on him as her future husband.

As soon as he saw Poveretta, on whom all eyes were turned, he stood still, struck with admira-

tion, and hardly daring to breathe. He did not
know her at first, for he had not seen her since
her father's death, at which time she had seemed
to him an insignificant child. But, seeing her in
company with Barbara and the fairy, who was
well known at court, he soon remembered her
name, and approached the ladies with an eager
politeness, which greatly flattered Barbara. You
can imagine her astonishment when the prince
bowed respectfully to her sister, and asked her to
dance.

"He thinks to please me by inviting this child,
whom no one wants as a partner," thought
the haughty Barbara. Absorbed in her painful
thoughts, she had seen nothing that was passing
around her.

Meanwhile the young prince had led away Poveretta. In the intervals of the dance he talked in
a tender voice of their childish sports, and fixed
on her a loving gaze that troubled the poor child.
"What a good husband for my sister!" thought she.

As he led her to a seat he timidly expressed a
wish to dance with her again. "When you have
danced with my sister, and not before," said she,
laughing. "Look around," added she, with childish innocence, "and see if there is any one here
that can equal her."

The prince was on the point of replying by one

of those compliments which are so easily found when we do not think them, much more when we do; but respect for the innocent child restrained him. He raised his eyes to Barbara, and, though the comparison was wholly in her sister's favor, he could not deny that she was really beautiful. Her face, indeed, had changed, and she was herself again. On seeing Poveretta carry off the prince, whom she thought her property, she had been seized with frantic terror. It seemed to her that some misfortune was about to happen, and that the poverty of her sister's dress was on the point of being exposed.

"They are capable of blaming me for it, and despising me on the account," said she. This thought, added to those which already disturbed her, almost drove her distracted. She finally made a desperate resolution. "It is very good of me to leave these rags on her back, and be tormented in this way, when I have more new dresses than I know what to do with," thought she. "In future I will dress her like myself."

The fairy, who was watching her, smiled, for she read her soul; and at the same instant Barbara felt relieved from the weight that oppressed her; she was free again to enjoy her splendid dress, and to abandon herself to the pleasure of the ball.

The prince, like a well-bred man, danced by turns with the two sisters, and was very attentive to the fairy, who was also an old acquaintance, and who had given him many a toy while he was still in frocks. He laughed heartily with Barbara on recalling the old stories in which they had both taken part; but if he talked more to the elder, he looked more at the younger, who listened with innocent delight. It seemed to her now that it would have been a great pity to have missed this ball, which she had valued so cheaply; she had never been so happy in her life.

They lingered as late as possible, for Barbara enjoyed the ball as much as Poveretta, and the good fairy, delighted at her goddaughter's success, was in no haste to leave. They were forced, however, at last to depart. The dawn was already gilding the horizon, and the wearied tapers refused to burn in the heavy air of the ballroom. It was the close of winter. A cold blast was sweeping through the streets, and the roofs of the houses were silvered by the hoar-frost. Barbara carefully wrapped herself in a large cloak lined with the finest fur. Poveretta, who had nothing of the kind, began to shiver in her thin dress as soon as she felt the cold air; but her godmother took her in her arms, and kept her warm in her pelisse during the ride, which was not long, thanks to the deer.

On going to her room, the mistress of the house found a large fire which had been kept up all night, and hastily held her cold feet near the blaze. But, strange to say, instead of finding any heat, she grew colder and colder, till her whole body was benumbed and her teeth chattered violently. It was in vain for her to ring and order logs to be heaped on the hearth; the fire had no effect on her, and her chilled fingers refused her all service, while at the same time an inner voice, which she vainly tried to stifle, cried out to her, " Your sister is cold !" Terrified at last, and weary of this persecution, she inquired the way to her sister's room, and climbed the stairs to it for the first time.

The servants, accustomed to neglect Poveretta, had not taken the trouble to build a fire in her chamber, and the delicate little creature had been seized with a chill on beginning to undress. Barbara found her shivering, her hands and lips blue with cold. She shouted for the servants, who ran thither trembling. " How is it," she cried, " that there is no fire in this room ? Would you have me die of cold ?"

The servants did not exactly understand her meaning, but it was easy to see that she wanted fire. They hastened with the ludicrous eagerness of servants in fault, and in less than two minutes a clear and sparkling blaze lighted up the desolate chamber of Poveretta, who knew not how to thank her sister. But Barbara did not listen; she was no longer cold, and that was enough for her.

"This is becoming unendurable," murmured she, on returning to her apartments. "Is this little fool always to spoil my life in this way? Oh, how I detest her!" And she went to bed, her soul harrowed by bitter resentment. Poveretta had just fallen asleep with a smile on her lips, repeating to herself how kind her sister had been to her.

At three o'clock in the afternoon Barbara rose from her bed, where she had found great difficulty in sleeping, and went with real pleasure to the dining-room, for she had eaten nothing nourishing since the evening before, and was very hungry.

Poveretta had risen long since. Her first glance on awakening fell on the rich clothes which her sister, on returning from the ball, had ordered to be carried to her chamber. She cried out with surprise, and, it must be confessed, was very happy, on putting them on, to see herself so well dressed. I know not whether the memory of the ball made her more attentive to her toilet; it is certain that she fell into a fit of musing, and heaved a little sigh at the thought that she had nothing, and could scarcely dream of marrying.

The gnawings of her stomach finally recalled her to other thoughts, and she was forced to confess that she would have gladly eaten something. But the servants, furious at her for the scene of the morning, had purposely forgotten her, and as she had lost the habit of giving them any orders, she patiently resigned herself to necessity, saying, by way of consolation, "I should soon have my dinner if my sister knew it."

In the mean time Barbara had taken her seat at her little table, where the most delicious dinner that could be imagined was awaiting her. A savory turtle-soup was smoking in a silver tureen, with a fillet of lamb with cream sauce on the right, and a dish of broiled ortolans on the left. A fine salmon trout was in the background, leaving just room enough for a cream of the most inviting appearance. We should say nothing of the wines at a young lady's dinner; nevertheless there were several kinds, among others a bottle of choice Tokay, which would have excited the envy of critics. Barbara lived well, and suffered herself to want for nothing. It must be said, however, that the glasses were very small.

She sat down without more delay to do honor to the feast, but scarcely had she tasted the soup when she dropped the spoon, nauseated by its bitterness, while the same voice that she had already heard whispered in her ear, "Your sister is hungry." "Oh dear," said she, "I would wager that the stupid fool has not had her dinner. I wish that she was a hundred feet under ground!"

But, already taught by experience, she made no attempt to resist. She climbed the stairs to her sister's room, took her by the hand, and led her to dinner, after clearing a corner of the table as well as she could, in reward for which she found the soup excellent, and feasted as long as she liked.

This was not all; these two forced visits to the wretched chamber had poisoned all her pleasure in her mirrors, carpets, and easy-chairs, and, pursued every where by the image of the rickety table and broken chair, she could only find repose by giving orders in an angry voice to put her sister in a room adjoining her own, which would no longer disgrace her luxury.

Poveretta had therefore gained possession by force, as it were, of all that her sister ought to have given her of her own accord from the beginning. But she was still far from the happiness for which she was anxious above every thing— the love of Barbara. At each new concession made by the latter to the pitiless tyrant imposed on her by the fairy, she felt her hatred of Poveretta increase, and with the hatred her sufferings

grew greater and greater. The good little Poveretta did not observe her harsh air and evil glance,
and abandoned herself without restraint to her
joy. She saw herself brought in close compan-
ionship with her whom she loved so well; but
while the idea of living side by side with her sister filled her with delight, the same idea was intolerable torture to the wicked Barbara, who, pre-
tending to be tired from the fatigues of the past
night, sent her to bed as soon as it was evening.

Delivered at last from her sight, Barbara
stretched herself in an easy-chair, with her feet to
the fire, and her thoughts, by degrees, took another turn. She returned to the ball, and was recalling to memory her merry conversation with the
friend of her childhood, who had never appeared
to her so interesting, when the mother of him
who filled her thoughts was announced. She
blushed involuntarily, and ran to meet her.

The princess was an old lady of the highest re-
spectability, who lived in great retirement, and
never showed herself without a grave reason.
Her visit evidently had a purpose. What motive
could have brought her? Barbara was sure that
she knew.

The first greetings having been exchanged, "My
child," said the old lady, "you know that our fami-
lies have been allied by friendship for many years."

"It is an honor which we can not forget," answered Barbara, with a beating heart.

"You know my son. I will not praise him, but I can say that he is a man of honor."

"No one could doubt that, madam."

"He returned this morning from the ball so delighted with what he had seen that he could wait no longer to open his heart to me."

"And what great secret could he have confided to you, madam?" said Barbara, casting down her eyes.

"Would it please you, who are now the head of the family, to strengthen the bonds of friendship which unite us by an alliance?"

"Indeed, madam, I was far from expecting a proposal that does me honor. What can I answer except that I dare not offer you a refusal which might—"

"That is all I wished to know," interrupted the princess, rising. "I am happy, my child, to see you thus disposed. I beg you to inform your sister that my son asks her in marriage. He will come to-morrow to seek her consent."

With these words the old lady rose, leaving Barbara plunged in such astonishment that she did not even rise to accompany her to the door.

On recovering from her surprise, she was seized with a frenzy of rage that took away her reason, and, not knowing what she did, she caught up a Damascus dagger, an Eastern curiosity which was lying on the mantle-piece, and rushed like a fury to Poveretta's chamber, which was dimly lighted by a night-lamp.

The lovely child was sleeping sweetly, with her little hands clasped on the coverlet, as if she had fallen asleep in the midst of a prayer. The angelic sweetness of her face might have soothed a tiger, but, intoxicated with anger, Barbara did not stop to look at it. She threw herself upon her sister, and buried the dagger to the hilt in her breast.

She had scarcely drawn out the weapon, when, struck herself by an invisible hand, she fell lifeless on the floor. The fairy at the same moment appeared. Casting a disdainful look on the murderess, "Have you forgotten," said she, "that no calamity can happen to your sister without falling upon you?"

In the mean time Poveretta had been awakened by the noise of the fall alone, for she had not felt the wound, which had instantly healed of itself, not, however, without the loss of a few drops of blood which stained her night-dress. She started at the sight of the blood, and saw her godmother at the foot of the bed.

"Oh, godmamma, what is the matter?"

"Look, my child. I had punished your sister for her harsh treatment of you by inflicting on her the torments of hatred, and now she has met her death in trying to kill you. See, the dagger is still in her hand."

Poveretta threw herself on her sister's body, sobbing. "Oh, godmamma, what have you done?" she cried. "My happiness is gone forever if my sister has died on my account. In heaven's name, restore her to life, or I shall die." She clasped the lifeless body in her arms, and, inundating it with tears, tried to warm it with her kisses.

The fairy was conquered by such perfect self-forgetfulness. She laid her finger on Barbara, who opened her eyes.

"My poor darling," whispered Poveretta, "how could I have rendered you unhappy enough to make you wish to kill me?"

Barbara burst into tears, whether from the touch of the fairy, or this sublime goodness, or both together, and, throwing her feeble arms round her sister's neck, she said, in a trembling voice, "Forgive me!"

This was the end of Poveretta's misfortunes, if that name can be given to ills which scarcely touched her, protected as she was by the impenetrable buckler of her love. The prince came the next day, and had no difficulty in persuading her to

accept him, when Barbara herself had consented
to the marriage. Her self-love had suffered more
than her heart from the disappointment which
she had had, and it was not long before she con-
soled herself by listening to the proposal of a
young nobleman on whom she had long looked
with a favorable eye.

What more can I tell you? The two sisters
were married on the same day, and cherished each
other with a reciprocal tenderness as long as they
lived. Barbara still remembered, when she was
an old grandmother, the torments which she had
formerly endured, and the terrible scene which
had ended them.

"Ah!" said she one day to her sister, who came
to see her with her two golden-haired little daughters, "may these children never know hatred between sisters! May they be convinced in after
life that we can not be happy by the side of the
unfortunate, and that it is almost selfish to be
kind to others!"

K

THE MAD COW.

ONCE upon a time there was in a village a great, ugly, lean, dirty, cross-grained cow, with crooked horns, that frightened every body. She had made her appearance suddenly, one winter's day, just after a great wedding, at which the guests had sat for three days and nights at the table, only rising now and then to dance. A poor laboring man, who was at the wedding, reeled home with her, without troubling himself much about whence she came, and she had a hard life with him. He made her work all day, sometimes at plowing up a field full of stones, and sometimes at carting dung for the rich peasants. At evening he sent her to seek her food along the road, where she found nothing but coarse, muddy, unsavory grass, and at night he shut her up in a wretched hovel, open to the winds, which was never cleaned, and which exhaled an infectious odor. With all this she was milked four times a day—just double what is required of cows bountifully fed, that live in idleness, and lodged in good, warm, clean stables.

Now this unhappy cow was nothing less than

a fairy—the fairy Good Appetite, the godmother of the bride at the wedding where the guests had eaten so much. The other fairies, indignant at such gluttony, had metamorphosed her in this manner to punish her for having in some sort authorized the feasting by her presence, and her present bad cheer was an expiation of the fault. To leave her some hope, she had been told that she should resume her original shape whenever she had reformed a thoroughly bad child. With this design, a part of her former power had been left her. She was permitted to do what she liked with the child, but she had no power over his heart; he must change of himself; and again, in token of his reformation, he must give her a hearty kiss between the horns: this would break the enchantment.

There was no lack of bad children in the village. In school-hours the streets were full of little vagrants, playing a thousand tricks on the passers-by, for the country was not yet wholly civilized, and it appeared a very natural thing in those days not to send children to school. You may imagine how the cow eyed them as she passed. Many times already she had made her choice among them, and chased them so furiously that, although her master had called her Misery because of her leanness and wretched appearance,

she was known throughout the country by the
name of the Mad Cow.

The little vagabonds, however, were nimble,
and too much accustomed to her sight to be afraid
of her. When she tried to catch them they sprang
familiarly on her back, clung to her horns, and
laughed so good-naturedly that she had no power
over them. To tell the truth, none of them was
altogether wicked. Amid all their badness, they
had their good traits—fidelity to each other, courage, and a sense of honor in certain things; and
as soon as Dame Misery came close to them, she
saw that they would not answer her purpose.

At last, toward the middle of spring, the lord
of the village made his entry with six carriages,
on the way to his castle, bringing with him his
whole family. He was a rich and powerful man,
but Heaven had afflicted him with a little boy
such as, happily, is not often found.

In the first place, he would learn nothing, fancying that learning was only for the common people, and that a young lord like him would be dis-
graced by study, to say nothing of its being very
tiresome. Next, and what was much worse, he
despised every body; he looked on his father's
servants as something between noblemen and the
brutes, and took for beggars all who did not
wear embroidered clothes, with swords at their

side. Moreover, he acted as though the world had been created expressly for him, never troubled himself about any thing or any one, and took whatever he pleased, wherever he found it, as if it had been his property. Lastly, and this was the most abominable of all, he did not even love his parents, and had for them neither gratitude nor respect; he did not deign to listen when they spoke to him, and obeyed them only when he pleased. With all this, he was too cowardly to bear pain, and too effeminate to endure fatigue, refusing to walk as soon as his feet hurt him, as chattering as a magpie, a liar when occasion offered, and always a glutton, although he made a great fuss about eating soup and meat. From this you can form an idea what a charming child was little Zephyr, for that was the name which he had received on coming into the world, a name much too pretty for such a scamp.

On the very evening of his arrival, Zephyr took a fancy to show himself in all his glory to the people of the village. He went out, therefore, with his little sister, followed at a short distance by a tall footman, carrying the young lady's shawl. He walked proudly, with head erect, gracefully tossing the plumes in his felt hat, and cavalierly tapping his fine boots with a little cane surmounted by a golden apple. His pretty

black velvet frock was confined around the waist
by a belt of silk and gold, and a costly watch,
buried in his fob, showed the end of a chain artistically wrought, with a large bunch of Lilipu-
tian charms, each one of which had cost as much
as ten sacks of potatoes. The village children
opened their eyes wide on seeing him pass, and
one of them, having had the audacity to approach
him in order to gain a better sight of all these
fine things, received a smart blow in the face
from the gold-headed cane, to which he made no
reply, so much was he terrified by the sight of
the tall footman.

The Mad Cow at that moment was seeking her
supper in the ditches along the road. As soon as
she saw the little gentleman in the distance, she
knew at once that he was just what she was looking for. His little sister was not much better,
but the reformation of one was sufficient to break
the spell of the poor fairy. Rushing forward, she
reached Zephyr just as he turned to the crying
child, and said to him, in an insolent tone,

"This will teach you, my boy—"

He had not time to say more. Suddenly bending her head, the cow lifted him from the ground
on her horns, to which he clung instinctively, and
carried him off at an incredible speed, while the
plumed hat and the gold-headed cane rolled in

the road. Too badly brought up to have any
pity for the accident that had happened to a
young gentleman so quick to strike, the naughty
little peasants burst into loud shouts of laughter,
and ran to pick up what he had lost. The tall
footman rushed after him; but an ox might as
well have tried to overtake a locomotive; and
that night they went to bed at the castle without the heir.

In the mean time the Mad Cow still ran on,
asking herself what she should do with the wicked boy.

"The reason that he is so bad," thought she,
"is that his parents have spoiled him by their

tenderness. I will not drive him to despair by making too great a change in his mode of life. It will suffice, perhaps, for him no longer to have his father and mother at hand, to teach him to reflect within himself, and to learn to know the world."

After dashing like lightning past cities and villages, swimming rivers, and crossing mountains at one bound, she laid him down gently on the lawn of a beautiful castle, even finer than that of his father.

Night had set in, and the lady of the castle was walking in the park with her husband to enjoy the cool air, holding by the hand her little boy of nearly the same age as Zephyr. All three were good people, benevolent to every one, and with no more pride than usually falls to the lot of mankind. Zephyr could easily have fallen into worse hands. When they saw him stretched almost senseless on the turf, they raised him up with great compassion.

"The poor child!" said the lady, "where can he have come from?"

"It is easy to see from his clothes," said the gentleman, "that he is of good family, though he is not dressed in the fashion of this country."

"Oh, mamma," said the little boy, "see! he is opening his eyes."

Zephyr, who had been stunned from the beginning by the rapidity of the flight, recovered his senses under the gentle hands of the lady, and, thinking himself at home, cried out abruptly,

"Where are my hat and cane?"

"It is true," said the lady, "the poor boy is bareheaded. Sylvan, go and bring him one of your old caps."

While Sylvan was gone in search of the cap, the gentleman and his wife questioned Zephyr, who gave his own and his father's names, but the cow had carried him so far that, to his great astonishment, these names had never been heard of in the country where he found himself. They asked him the name of the village in which his castle was situated. He told it as well as he could, but it was a name difficult to pronounce, and as he had never taken the trouble to learn it correctly, it was impossible to find it by looking on the map. He told how the cow had carried him off on her horns, and the story was received with a smile that humiliated him greatly.

"Wherever he may come from, we will keep him, my dear," said the good lady; "he will amuse our little Sylvan, who has no playfellow."

"His story appears to me a little suspicious," answered her husband; "but no matter, my love, if it pleases you, I shall make no objection."

And thus, received through charity, poor Zephyr was taken to the castle, and sent to sleep in a little room under the roof.

"Master and mistress are always looking for something to give us trouble," grumbled the old nurse who led him to his new abode. "They seem to think that we have not work enough on our hands, that they must burden themselves with a little vagabond, come from no one knows where."

"Insolent wretch," cried the young lord, purple with anger, "how dare you speak in that way to me? I command you to be silent!"

"You are a fine blade to command me to do any thing. Come, go in there; it is too good for you; and take care to be polite to me, if you don't want to bear the marks of my fingers!"

And the old woman pushed him into the room with a hearty cuff which he was forced to bear, for she instantly shut the door and turned the key in the lock.

Zephyr had great difficulty in sleeping, worn out though he was by the journey which he had made in a somewhat uncomfortable position. For the first time in his life he had experienced humiliation, and the recollection of the contempt which he had so often lavished on others weighed a little on his conscience. But his pride was not subdued, and his only gratitude toward those who had given him an asylum was to fall asleep abusing them in his heart.

The next morning Sylvan rose at daybreak, such was his haste to become acquainted with his new playfellow, and gave his mother no rest till she sent the old nurse for the little stranger. He was sleeping soundly when she entered, and was by no means pleased at Sylvan's invitation to rise at once and take a walk.

"Let him take his walk without me," grumbled he; "I don't want to get up."

"What! do you think that you are going to eat master's bread for nothing? The dear child does you too much honor, indeed, in wishing for your company. I should like to see you keep him waiting!"

She seized him without ceremony, drew on his trowsers, and gave him his first lesson in rising early when he wished to sleep. He was furious; however, he had the sense to face misfortune bravely, and went down stairs to Sylvan, who welcomed him with delight. The morning was beautiful, and the park enchanting, and Zephyr, who was not in the habit of seeing the sun rise, was not sorry to witness this magic spectacle, of which the indolent do very wrong to deprive themselves.

At that age vexation is quickly forgotten;

their play soon commenced to the general satisfaction. The good little Sylvan did the honors as well as he could, and brought all his pretty things to show his new friend. Unluckily, his eyes fell on the gay silk belt, embroidered with gold, which Zephyr wore about his waist, and as he had a weakness for every thing bright, he took a violent fancy to it. Zephyr decidedly refused the proposal to exchange it for a patent-leather belt, and Sylvan cried to his mother, who happened to be passing at that moment, "Mamma, he will not give me his belt."

"Yes he will, my dear," answered the lady, who could refuse her child nothing, " he will give it to you, for you gave him your cap yesterday." She went on, without thinking any more about the matter. But the pitiless old nurse, who was sweeping before the door, had heard her words. Exasperated at seeing the little beggar, as she called him, oppose Master Sylvan, who was her idol, she sprang upon the belt, the object coveted by her darling, and in the twinkling of an eye snatched it from Zephyr.

This should have taught him, it would seem, that it is just to respect the property of others; but he thought little about that. Feeling that before the house he would be the weaker, he led Sylvan, whose tears were soon dried, to the bottom of the park; then, when he was sure that no one could see him, he fell upon the child, and beat him soundly, to force him to give back the belt.

He was about to triumph, when suddenly a pair of long pointed horns were thrust between the combatants, and Zephyr, carried away anew by the cow, resumed his journey around the world with a rapidity that turned his brain.

"Decidedly," said the Mad Cow, "castle life is worth nothing to him. If I put him in trade he will have a more busy life."

And, leaping over the walls of a great city, she tossed him without ceremony on a pile of bales, before the door of a small shop-keeper, then fled in haste, for the women were already coming out of the houses with their brooms, and the police-men were running to put her into the pound, thinking her some peasant's cow escaped from the market.

"What are you doing there, you young vaga-bond?" cried the shop-keeper, a little, plump, red-faced man, who, with his spectacles on his nose, and his invoices in his hand, was carefully exam-ining the number and contents of the bales.

And two fingers, which were none of the soft-est, vigorously tweaked the ear of the fainting boy, who speedily recovered his senses.

"Oh, sir!" he exclaimed, clasping his hands,

"do not hurt me. It was the cow that threw me here."

He told his story with somewhat less assurance, it is true, than he had told it the first time. The shop-keeper shook his head, with a significant laugh.

"Do you expect a business man like me to believe such stuff?" said he. "No matter; since you are here, I will keep you. Go into the house, and I will talk with my wife about it."

The shop-keeper's wife protested loudly when her husband informed her that he intended to keep the child. But he was a man that would have his own way, and what he said, he did. He condescended, however, to explain to her that they were just then in need of an apprentice to do errands and tend the shop when they were busy with something else, and that here was one ready to their hand, who would cost nothing, and whom they would not do a bad thing to take. It cost nothing to keep an urchin like that, and it was an easy matter to put a mattress for him in the shop-loft, by the side of the barrels of salt cod.

"Besides," he added, "you see that he is dressed like a young lord, and in a fashion that, on my word, is quite original. We will let him carry Anthony's books to school, and it will do us credit in the town."

This last argument convinced his wife, who was as vain as she was avaricious; and as she passed the dress of her new apprentice in review with a jealous eye, she perceived the chain and charms, which indicated the presence of a watch in the fob.

"I want to know," she exclaimed, "whether there is any sense in putting jewelry like that on a child of his age?" And, to revenge the insult to good sense, she laid hands on the chain, and brought away the watch and charms.

"It is very pretty," said the shop-keeper, examining his wife's capture, "and I dare say cost a great deal of money. We will let Anthony wear it when he has his Sunday clothes on."

The sentence passed, the prey was carefully put away in a drawer as a lawful prize, and nothing more was said about it. No provision for such a case having been made by the Board of Trade, the conscience of the pair was completely at rest.

Zephyr entered at once upon his duties. A broom was put into his hands, and he was made to sweep the house from top to bottom.

The poor child was struck dumb. His heart was bursting with indignation, but he felt himself defenseless against such crushing misfortune. The harsh manner in which he had been recalled to his senses had subdued his rebellious spirit, and his smarting ear warned him that it was of no use to attempt resistance.

This was, however, the only treatment of the kind that he experienced. The shop-keeper had used this brutality only because he thought his merchandise in danger, the only point on which he was savage; apart from this he was not ill-natured. Provided that his little business went on

to suit him, he wished harm to no one. He even
went so far as to desire happiness for the whole
human race, so that it cost him nothing. When
the apprentice reappeared in the court-yard, his
broom in hand, he tweaked his ear anew, but this
time softly, and said, in a good-natured tone,

"Courage, my little man. This is the way that
I began, and you see what I am now. Work
hard, and who knows? perhaps some day you
may hold the same station that I do."

The worthy man thought his station a high
one, and looked up to no one in the world.

Under this somewhat gentle but inflexible dis-
cipline, Zephyr began to amend. To lie abed late
in the morning was not even to be thought of,
and, in fact, he did not think about it. Always
on his feet, and always with something to do, he
had not time to remember himself, and by degrees
lost sight of his important little person. Once or
twice, indeed, he attempted to put on his lofty
airs with the people who came to the shop, but
his master, who could not be polite enough to his
customers, having let him know that at the next
offense he should go to bed without his supper,
which would be a clear gain to the house, he understood that it was a thing which he had better
not do, and never repeated it. He sat at the table with his employers, and, as the table was

round, one seat was as good as another; but, the soup and meat once eaten, he had been taught to go into the shop to look after the customers, as much through economy as to keep him at a respectful distance. This gave him an increasing respect for the soup and meat, formerly so much despised; and one day, when an apple that was beginning to spoil was thrown him, he thought that he had received a magnificent present. He was not maltreated, as we have said; but never did he receive a mark of attachment, a caress, or a friendly word, unless the shop-keeper thought fit to encourage him to *work hard*, an admonition for which he had a great liking. At night, when the poor child climbed laboriously to his musty garret, and stretched himself on his mattress, the remembrance of the tender kisses of his mother, which he had formerly received with such indifference, and the gentle voice of his father, to which he had scarcely listened, swelled his bosom, and he fell asleep sighing, with their dear images before his eyes.

The most disagreeable part of his position was the service which he was obliged to render to his master's son. Since Anthony had had a footman to carry his books to school, he would not have carried them himself for an empire; and, whatever little Zephyr was doing, he was forced to leave

it to carry the hateful package. Neither were
they friends, for Anthony was a boy that talked
with none but those of his own station, and would
not even permit the little porter to walk by his
side. On seeing him march proudly three steps
in advance, Zephyr could form an idea of the air
that he must have had in the days of the tall
footman.

Again, if the journey had been made directly,
he would have soon seen the end of it; but Anthony was a good-for-nothing fellow, who cared
little for school or for any thing else. He loved
nothing but marbles, and thought only of pro-
curing as many of them as he could by every
possible means.

Some distance at the right of the school-house
was a little square, where all the wealthiest part
of the truant population assembled in class-hours.
This was the great marble market, where flour-
ished pitch and toss, and all the games by which
boys could gain or lose; there were negotiated
exchanges and sales, and there was settled the
rise and fall of agates. Master Anthony went
regularly twice a day to this place to serve his
apprenticeship to trade. He called it his Exchange, precocious child as he was, and sometimes staid there whole hours, absorbed in his
speculations. During all this time the little

porter remained on his feet, awaiting the good pleasure of the young broker, who never permitted him to put down his books till he reached the school-room door, which was very allowable, since his parents' means permitted him to keep a servant.

Zephyr had full time to recollect how he too had often kept servants on their feet for whole hours for the most idle reasons; but as these remembrances were not sufficient to kill the time, he finally took it into his head, as a last resource, to open the unhappy books, the source of his slavery, and, though they were not very amusing, by degrees he acquired a taste for them, so that it was Anthony who went to school, and Zephyr who learned the lessons.

"Anthony," said one of his playfellows one day, "do you see your groom using your books?"

"Let him read, poor wretch! he needs it to make his way in the world. How much for a hundred agates?"

Three months passed in this manner. The former nobleman had already gained much. Nevertheless, the power which he had won over himself was not yet of the right kind. Fear alone inspired him, and selfishness still dwelt at the bottom of his heart, and was only silenced. At last, one fine morning, when the marble market

was more brisk than usual, and the session threatened to be indefinitely prolonged, he was seized
with an irresistible fancy to be his own master
for a moment. He put the books under his arm,
and, without saying a word, took the way to the
city gate, leaving the idle Anthony to his com-
mercial speculations.

It was one of those beautiful autumnal morn-
ings when the sun seems to gaze at the earth with
a loving eye, as if bidding it farewell. On crossing the city walls, the child breathed with delight the fresh breeze as it shook a leaf from time
to time from the still green trees. He gazed at
the country, and stooped to pick a flower with a
feeling wholly new to him, so long had he seen
nothing but pavements, and been pursued by the
odor of salt cod.

What was his astonishment to see the Mad
Cow in a pasture by the road side looking at him
with a melancholy eye. His first impulse was to
take flight; but the misfortunes of his life had already developed his courage. He walked straight
toward her.

"What do you want with me?" said he, without shrinking "If it is to take me away from
here, you are welcome to do so; I have had
enough of this kind of life."

All the humiliations to which he had submitted

for the last three months rose before his eyes like an army at these words, and he vowed within himself never again to set foot in that hateful shop. The ingrate did not yet feel all that he owed to it.

"If I carry you elsewhere, you will have many besides yourself to support, my poor boy!" answered the cow.

"No matter, it will be different. Any thing rather than be for a minute longer the servant of that Anthony!"

Zephyr was beginning to have courage. He bravely seized the horns, by the means of which he had already traveled so far, and, lifting him on her back, the cow set out on a gentle trot.

They had become acquaintances, and this journey was more sociable than the preceding ones.

"You do not go very fast to-day," said Zephyr to his steed, as she stopped from time to time, and bent her long, lean neck to snatch a tuft of grass.

"Oh, I am in no haste. We have not far to go."

"I am beginning to be hungry."

"Well, drink some of my milk."

The little boy leaped to the ground, and, clinging to the udder of the Mad Cow, drank her milk greedily. He found it of an acrid flavor, which was not, however, disagreeable. It was strengthening, though not nourishing, and when he mounted again he felt his heart lightened, and looked at the future without great anxiety.

She carried him in this manner all day, along the hedges and through the meadows, where the hay of the late harvest was piled up in fragrant stacks. He drank in the pure air, and broke forth into bursts of song, which would have greatly astonished his poor parents could they have seen him thus mounted, going he knew not where. When evening came he began to think of them, their tenderness and their sorrow, and a tear rolled down his cheek, already slightly browned, as he asked himself when and how he could return to them. He was decidedly becoming better.

Night came, and the cow still went on. At last she stopped before a poor solitary cabin, at the entrance of a wood, with a great dung-heap before the door. Zephyr could just discern by the light of the stars its thatched roof, half broken in, and dented in places with great tufts of moss, and the worm-eaten board fence which inclosed a bit of tilled ground adjoining the house.

"This is the place," said she; "get down and go in."

"Here! you can not be in earnest; it is too dirty."

"Get down, I tell you, and go in. I will go with you, and never quit you again."

Despite his newly-born friendship for the Mad Cow, the prospect which she offered him was not inviting enough to persuade him to accept it, and he clung fast to her horns, by no means delighted by her proposition. She made a sudden spring which unloosed his hold, and threw him his whole length on the dung-heap.

At the noise of his fall a great dog rushed barking from the cabin, and a homely peasant-woman appeared at the door.

"Who is there?" said she. "What do you want at this hour?"

"Can you take me into your house, my good lady?" said Zephyr, in a timid voice, rising, and attempting to wipe the dirt from his clothes.

"Begone quickly, you little vagabond! Do you take my house for an inn? Come, John, and see the little gentleman who wants to lodge here."

Zephyr had taken refuge behind his cow, to escape the dog, which was barking furiously, and threatening to bite him.

"You must stay here," whispered she.

The peasant appeared with a lantern. He was a tall, powerful man, with a stern look, and strongly-marked features.

"I have no room for vagabonds. Go your

way, you and your unlucky cow, or it will be worse for you."

Zephyr fell on his knees. "For pity's sake, my good sir," said he. He had not time to say more. A large boy, scarcely any older, but twice as strong as he, rushed from the cabin, and, taking the supplicant in his arms,

"I want the little gentleman myself," cried he. "I want him to come and live with us."

John and his wife looked at each other, and felt that they must yield.

"Well," said the subjugated father, "come in, then, to please Jack."

The door closed on them, and the Mad Cow took her way of her own accord to a dilapidated stable, where a little one-eyed horse, with long, matted hair, was sadly nibbling a remnant of old litter.

As had been foretold to Zephyr, he led a harder life than he had done with the shop-keeper, but there is reason to believe that he suffered less.

As a beginning, the very next morning the peasant's wife took off every article of clothing that he had on when he arrived. The velvet frock had received more than one spot in the shop and the city, and bore traces of his recent encounter with the dung-heap, but, such as it was, it was the admiration of the whole cabin. The peasant-woman cleaned it as well as she could, brushed it, and put it away with the rest in a corner of the chest of drawers.

"It is much too fine for this place, and I don't want it to be worn out here," said she. "It will be ready for him when he goes away." She gave him a coarse shirt, a pair of cotton trowsers, a blue blouse, and a pair of wooden shoes, all borrowed from Jack's best wardrobe. He had no stockings, indeed, yet this was not from avarice, or to make a distinction between him and the son of the house. He was among honest people, difficult of approach, it is true, harsh to others as well as to themselves, and keeping both their heart and their hands tightly shut; but when once they had opened them, they gave all that was within.

Poor Zephyr at first felt uncomfortable in his new costume. His delicate limbs were lost in big Jack's clothes, and the wooden shoes seemed very hard to his little bare feet. He put a large handful of fresh straw in them, and two days after he thought no more of it.

When the time came to sit down to the table there was a fresh hardship. The feast consisted wholly of black bread and potatoes, and it must be confessed that Zephyr made a grimace at the first mouthful. Fortunately, the milk that he had drank the night before had sharpened his appetite. Moreover, as he was hospitably treated, and was not sent away at dessert, he was not very unhappy. In a few days it was the same with the black bread as with the shoes — he thought it excellent.

Both room and furniture were scanty in the cabin, and the bed that was given Jack's guest was not magnificent. It was a truss of hay in the stable with the animals. But how different from his loft in the city! Here, at least, he had pure air, and that healthful stable odor which cures invalids. When he threw himself half undressed on his couch, the cow, become his warm friend, stretched her nose to him for a caress, the dog licked his hands, and even the little one-eyed horse gave him a friendly look. How sweetly he slept at night, and how briskly he rose in the morning! Too good beds make you indolent; they hold you tight in their coverings, and will not let you go. How often, when he waked before dawn, and leaned on his elbow, watching the sleeping animals—how often his thoughts carried him back to the sumptuous castle that he had lost. Yet it was no longer of its splendors that he dreamed, but of the good parents whom he had left there; and this recollection of the past did not torture him as before, for he felt that he was becoming better, and something told him that he would be rewarded.

He soon grew familiar with people as well as things. John had at first frightened him with his loud voice and stern glance. He did not always use the softest words to express his wishes, and Anthony's father was gentler in his language. But there was a sort of native dignity and authority in the tall peasant that rendered it easy to obey him, because obedience seemed natural, and his honest rudeness strengthened the child's soul while startling it. Zephyr was not long in feeling toward him that affectionate respect, unmixed with fear, which is inspired by strong and candid natures, and which does children so much good when they are made to feel it.

John's wife was not handsome, and she also

was somewhat loud-tongued; but she conceived such an affection for the child that she called him nothing but her darling, and she was so good to him that, in spite of her scolding, he could not help loving her with all his heart. Happy is he who loves some one! If fear is the beginning of wisdom, love is the beginning of goodness.

Jack, his protector, was at first his only serious vexation. Without thinking himself an inch taller than the wearer of his blouse and trowsers, he innocently took advantage of his strength to tease the little gentleman, whose language and manners seemed to him ridiculously polished. The parents had not asked the boy his story through delicacy, but Jack knew it the very next morning. He laughed at it immoderately, and christened him at once the little *lord of the cow.* The name appeared so happy to him that he constantly repeated it, and in the end it became terribly disagreeable to Zephyr.

I was once at a menagerie where the keeper abandoned an unfortunate white kitten to the tender mercies of a huge monkey. The monkey stroked the kitten, boxed its ears, rolled it on the ground, let it go, caught it again, and held it up first by the tail, next by the head, and then by the middle of the body, while the poor kitten dared make no resistance, so much was it cowed by this constant persecution.

In the same way, Zephyr was at first in the hands, I had almost said the paws, of big Jack. He was less indignant than with Anthony, for, after all, he and Jack were comrades. The plays, however, were too rough for him, and the parents laughed at them, thinking it no harm. In the end, however, he summoned up all his energy, and, after three useless warnings to his tyrant, planted a blow with all his strength just between his eyes. Jack drew back without returning it, not that he cared much for the blow, but he had just learned that his sports were disagreeable to his friend — a thought which had not crossed his mind till that instant.

The little *lord of the cow* soon regained the advantage. The books which he had under his arm on quitting the city became a precious resource to him in this solitude. He was not long in learning all they could teach, and he then took it into his head to undertake the education of his sturdy playfellow, who tractably submitted, and began to show a high respect for him. All that Zephyr had not clearly understood while studying became plain to him when he was obliged to reflect seriously on it, in order to teach it. He gained himself thereby almost as much as his pupil, and learned, above all, the necessity of attention to study, by preaching it to his restless scholar, who could keep neither his mind nor his limbs in one place five minutes at a time. The lesson finished, Jack took his master's hand, and they bounded to the forest to look for bird's nests, watch the rabbits as they passed, and gather great armsful of dead branches, which they brought home in triumph for the winter.

They rendered each other service for service. A peasant would despise himself should he burden a child with hard work; but Jack was a proud boy, who could see no one do any thing before him without lending a hand, and as the two children never quitted each other, Zephyr learned to labor of his own accord. The little peasant taught the little gentleman how to handle a spade, roll a wheelbarrow, and load a cart. This amused him greatly, and he entered into it so heartily, that one day, as he was merrily digging up a piece of ground from which the onions had just been pulled up, John passed by, and, giving him a friendly slap on the shoulder, said,

"Courage, my boy, you are on the way to become a man!"

This simple speech made him six inches taller in his own estimation, which is a great deal for a little boy. He dropped his spade to breathe a little more freely, for he was almost stifling with self-satisfaction, and the Mad Cow, who was rambling about there, chancing at that moment to put her head through a gap in the old fence, he ran to her to caress her.

"Naughty cow," said he, "you have taken me away from my parents, but, in spite of that, I owe you too much to blame you for it." With these words he gave her a kiss between the horns.

A bright light suddenly dazzled him. A lady more beautiful than the day stood before him, and on looking down he saw himself dressed no longer in the ridiculous trappings of which he was formerly so proud, but in a simple, elegant, and convenient costume suited to a nobleman who is as yet nothing but a little child.

"You have saved us both," said the beautiful lady, clasping him in her arms. "Now bid farewell to your friends here; but be quick, for your parents are waiting for you."

It was a year to a day since the child had disappeared, and his parents, who still mourned as intensely as at the first moment, had shut themselves up in their room to give free vent to the tears called forth by this sad anniversary.

"Who will restore us our child?" said the mother, leaning her head on the shoulder of her husband, who was gazing at her with his eyes full of tears.

"Here he is," said the fairy, suddenly appearing before them with Zephyr.

I need not tell you what joy there was in the house. The mother frantically kissed her son again and again, and could not repeat often enough how tall and strong he had grown. The father saw with delight his frank and resolute air, his manly bearing, and the quiet simplicity of his manners. The servants ran thither without caring for etiquette, embracing every one they saw, and the tall footman, who had not dared to show himself since the fatal accident, fell into a chair and sobbed like a child.

"But what have you done with the Mad Cow?" asked the little sister, who could not recognize her brother.

"We have eaten her," said the fairy Good Appetite, laughing, and showing a magnificent set of teeth.

The fatted calf was killed, and the way in which Zephyr did honor to it gave reason to believe that the fairy had spoken the truth.

Since that time, in France, whenever a child is naughty, his parents threaten to make him eat the Mad Cow. Would that such children might all make her acquaintance, and that it might do them as much good as it did little Zephyr.

THE HOME FAIRY.

There was once a rich man who awakened one fine morning and found himself poor. He had long held a high rank in the world, and mixed only with lords and princes, but, his riches having taken flight, he was forced to retire to a wretched little village with his daughter Blanche, a beautiful young lady, who had been accustomed from her childhood to live in idleness, and who was very unhappy in her new habitation.

This was a miserable hovel, with smoky walls, low windows with little dingy panes, and an immense fireplace covered with soot. The ceiling, hung with spider's webs, was roughly coated with a thick layer of mortar, peeling off here and there, and resting on great rafters, blackened and cracked by age. The floor was nothing but rough, uneven earth, trodden hard and sprinkled with stones. A country road, broken up by the heavy cart-wheels, and full of yellow, sticky mud, interspersed with puddles of water, ran in front of the door, and around the hovel lay a piece of waste ground, choked up with weeds and thistles, and only separated from the potato-patch by a ruined wall.

You can judge whether such a dwelling could please people who had always lived in a splendid castle, with a crowd of servants ready to answer their call. Here, their only domestic was a poor old woman, called old Betty, partly deaf, and blind of one eye, who did their little cooking after her fashion, and pretended to keep in order the earthen dishes, old linen, and dilapidated furniture of the hovel. Like almost all the country people, she had her own cottage and piece of ground, and thought that she was doing them a great favor in consenting to take charge of their household, which no one else would undertake.

Poor Blanche, as I have said, found herself very unhappy. She would have given a great deal to have had her piano, but it was not to be thought of. She had brought away with her a piece of needlework, commenced in better days, with which she seated herself by the side of her father during the long hours, and strove from time to time to cheer the old man's gloomy face by all the merry speeches she could devise, which was a hard task, for her thoughts were by no means merry ones. But her painful efforts were not crowned with success. There comes an age when it is impossible to change one's habits, and if the young girl, full of life and health, grieved at her change of fortune, I leave you to think what must have been the trouble of this poor infirm old man, whose weak stomach revolted at the unskillful preparations of their new cook.

His life, therefore, was nothing but a continual complaint. The bread was badly baked and full of bran; the meat dry and burnt. The soup tasted of the vessel in which it was cooked. The windows let in the wind and shut out the light. The chimney smoked, but did not heat. Every thing in the house was dirty and out of order. Never was there so slovenly and neglectful a woman as old Betty.

To all these complaints the old woman, who had always been mistress at home, gave sharp answers, and it was not easy to have the last word with her. Blanche sometimes tried to interfere, either to quiet her father or to put a stop to the old woman's tongue, but with little success. All that she usually gained by it was a rebuff from her father, or an impertinent speech from the old woman.

One morning the old man woke in worse humor than usual. The covering had fallen off his bed during the night, and he had slept badly; his head was heavy and his eyes swollen, and he was furious with the old woman.

"Betty," said he, as soon as she entered, "how many times have I told you to tuck in the clothes better, and to turn back the coverlet at the head of the bed? You pay no attention to what I tell you, and, thanks to you, I have passed a wretched night."

"Dear papa," said Blanche, who saw a storm coming, "were you not restless last night? The bed seemed to me very well made."

"No," he answered, in a gruff tone, "no, miss, I was not restless, and if you had much consideration for your father, you would not take that woman's part against me. I ought to know best, I think, whether my bed was well made or not."

"What!" said the old woman, planting herself, with arms a-kimbo, before him, "do you think I have waited for you to teach me how to make a bed? I tell you that my own way is the right one, and I shall not change it at my age. My poor husband, who was worth two of you, was contented with it for thirty-five years, and you will have to be the same."

It was a little hard, you may imagine, to hear such language after having all your life been treated with the greatest deference. While the poor old man, purple with anger and indignation, stood vainly seeking for an answer, Blanche, provoked at such a want of respect, rose suddenly, and, taking Betty by the arm, turned her toward the little corner that served as a kitchen.

"Enough of this," said she; "go get your breakfast ready."

Her eyes sparkling with anger, and her commanding air, overawed the old woman, who did not attempt to resist. She hobbled away to her furnace, and muttered between her teeth loud enough for them to hear, as she was kindling her fire, "If they are not satisfied, let her do it herself. Fine airs for Jack and his daughter!"

You must know that, humiliated at having fallen so low, and full of contempt for the humble surroundings to which they were condemned, neither the father nor daughter had told any one their names, which made the villagers very angry. In great cities no one pays any attention to a new neighbor, but in villages it is very different. There the subjects for conversation are few, and when a good one occurs it is not readily suffered to drop. There was surely some mystery about a gentleman coming suddenly in this way from the city, with a young lady who kept her lofty airs in spite of her threadbare gown; and not even to tell their names was to wrong the curiosity of their neighbors. To the spite of unsatisfied curiosity was added a bitter rancor for the contempt expressed by this obstinate silence.

The countryman does not like to be treated with scorn by those who come to live in his neighborhood—a very natural feeling, and shared by all the world. The village wit at last thought of a coarse joke which put them all in good humor.

There was a donkey in the village which carried the butter and eggs to market, and which, according to custom, was called Jack. The villagers determined that, since they knew of no other name for the new neighbor, they would give him that of the donkey, and, as it was also necessary to find a name for the young lady, they were christened Jack and his daughter. This was certainly very ungenerous, for none but the ignorant insult those in misfortune; but the villagers were ignorant, and did not pride themselves on their good manners.

Little harm would have been done had this coarse jest gone no farther than those who had invented it. Unhappily, the report had reached the ears of Blanche, who suffered cruelly, less for herself than for her father who was thus insulted. Fancy what must have been her grief and shame at hearing herself called by this hateful name in her own house in the presence of her father, who fortunately did not hear it, or he would have asked for an explanation, which old Betty in her present temper would not have been long in giving.

The breakfast naturally suffered from the scene that had just taken place. It was detestable. The old man rose from the table with a gloomy brow, and his daughter timidly seated herself by his side with her needle-work in her hand. Alas! she had just perceived that she had no more worsted, neither had she any money with which to buy it. Worsted work costs dear; it is not profitable, but ruinous when one is not rich. Blanche tried in vain to enter into conversation. Her advances were coldly received, and a short sentence soon convinced her that her father was tired of her company.

She rose, her heart filled with sorrow, and left the house without speaking. A little footpath, trodden almost dry in the mud by the passers-by, wound along the road. She entered it mechanically, and began to reflect on her sad fate. Doubtless the privations of her wretched mode of life were not indifferent to her, and the sudden change in her habits had caused her more than one sigh, but her thoughts were not on these; she saw with terror that her father was daily becoming more and more estranged from her—her father, formerly so tender and so good! She remembered how, when a little child, he had devoured her with kisses; how he loved to hold her on his lap, pass his fingers through her curls, and play and chatter with her; and how his eyes filled with tears at the least vexation she had, no matter how trifling. And in after years, when her poor mother had quitted them, and they were left alone together, with how much love he had surrounded her! Pleasure or business, he quitted every thing for his idolized daughter. A smile or a look obtained any thing from him; and though they were then poor, his eagerness to satisfy, and even to anticipate all the whims of his beloved despot, showed his affection. Now he looked at her unmoved, when her heart was bursting with sorrow, and, unhappy as he was, was even unwilling for her to comfort him. This was, above all, what cut her to the heart, for the good girl loved her father; she was ready to make any sacrifice for him, and the thought that she could do nothing to make his life easier was her bitterest grief.

Turning these things over in her mind, she reached the fountain, and, seating herself on the steps, burst into tears. She sobbed for a long time without being disturbed, for every body was in the fields at that hour. Relieved at last by the torrent of tears that she had shed, she wiped her eyes, and was about to rise, when a woman whom she had not perceived set her foot on the steps where she was seated.

This was a lady of noble bearing, as beautiful

as a queen, and richly dressed, the owner of the
castle that was seen a little way from the village.
She had at her command a whole army of servants, but work and exercise were to her a necessity, and she came herself to draw water in a little
bucket hooped with silver, which she carried
proudly on her shoulder with a grace and style
far exceeding the most elegant of the fine ladies
that sweep the side-walk with their robes. You
should have seen her in harvest-time going to the
fields with her maids, her golden sickle in her
hand. The roughest peasants respectfully stepped aside to let her pass, and never did a duchess
presented at court excite a murmur of admiration
like that which greeted the beautiful lady of the
castle when she returned at evening, mounted on
the great wagon laden with sheaves, her eyes
sparkling and her cheeks flushed, holding in her
arms some chubby child crowned with corn pop-
pies. Every thing succeeded with her; where
others gained hundreds of dollars, she gained
thousands, and where others spent thousands, she
spent hundreds. No one could understand why,
but the truth was that she was a fairy, only she
said nothing about it, in order not to make a
scandal in the country.

When she saw poor Blanche, scarcely recovered
from her sobs, wiping her eyes with her handker-

chief, wet with tears, she felt great pity for her,
and, setting down her bucket on the edge of the
fountain,

"What is the matter, my dear child," said she,
"that you weep in this manner?"

"Alas! madam, I weep because I am daily losing my father's love."

"Are you not the daughter of the man who has
lately settled here?"

"Yes, madam," replied Blanche, blushing, for
she thought of Jack, and did not doubt that the
story was known every where.

"Your father is very unhappy, then?"

"Oh! wretchedly unhappy; and it is this also
that grieves me, for I would gladly give my life
for him."

The beautiful lady smiled quietly. "You need
not do so much as that," said she. "Only promise to make use of the gift which I am about to
bestow on you: WHATEVER YOU TOUCH WITH
YOUR OWN HANDS SHALL REJOICE YOUR FATHER'S
HEART. Go and weep no more. You were his
daughter; you shall be his mother, and he will
love you with a love that you have never yet
known."

Saying this, she filled her tiny bucket with water, and putting it on her shoulder, walked away
with a light and airy tread, breathing around her

an aroma of strength and courage calculated to render valiant the most timid hearts.

Blanche felt herself transformed by the words of the fairy. Without waiting, she took the way back to the house, and this time it was with an indescribable feeling that she perceived the humble roof, the sight of which had so often made her shudder. A sacred duty awaited her there, and she was in haste to take advantage of the magic power bestowed on her hands by the fairy.

As she approached, a neighbor's child—a chubby, rosy-cheeked boy who was paddling with his bare feet in the mud—maliciously stuck out his tongue at her as she passed, crying, "Oh! there goes Jack's daughter." He even threw a stone at her, which splashed her as it fell; and his father, a great, strapping peasant, who was leaning against his door smoking a short pipe, chuckled insolently at the sight. But Blanche was too light-hearted to be angry. She cast on the child a look of gentle reproach, which shamed him. He ran to his father, who was ashamed in his turn. He took his pipe from his mouth, and, bowing awkwardly, said, "Don't mind him, miss; he means nothing."

Meanwhile the old man had been meditating in his own heart since his daughter had left him, and had repented of his injustice to her. He too had called to mind the past. Had he nothing to reproach himself with toward this poor child, whom he had brought up in luxury and idleness, and had accustomed to such care and tenderness, and who had just been thrown into so sad a life, without even finding a comforter and support in her father? The old love which had been paralyzed in his heart, benumbed by misfortune, suddenly awakened, and sent a glow through his whole being. He picked up the needle-work which she had let fall, and was gazing at it absently, his mind lost in the memories of the past, when Blanche entered. Without speaking a word, with one impulse they fell into each other's arms, and long remained clasped in a warm embrace. At that moment they forgot every thing—old Betty, the uncomfortable bed, and the miseries of the wretched hovel, which seemed to them full of light.

The young girl was the first to disengage herself from this blissful embrace, and, casting on her father a mischievous smile,

"This window is very dirty," said she; "let us see if I can clean it."

"Don't think of it, my dear child," cried he; "leave that to Betty."

And he tried to snatch from her the house-cloth, which she had already dipped into a basin

of water, but she held fast to it, eager to see her
hands at work.

"I can do it better than Betty, father.   You
shall see."

As she spoke she sprang lightly on a chair, and
in an instant the housecloth was at work.   She
passed it over the dingy panes with a firm, quick

hand, wet and rubbed them, and enjoyed with de
light the marvelous transformation which was ef

fected under her nimble fingers. It was not, however, till she had finished, and leaped from her
chair to see her work, that she and her father
knew the full extent of what she had done.

The window-panes shone like diamonds in
their frames, freshly painted and furnished with
pretty bronze fastenings, which defied the fury of
the winds. Blue damask curtains, which had
hung themselves up of their own accord, fell in
graceful folds on each side of the window, and a
beautiful ray of sunshine, sent by the fairy, suddenly illumined all this splendor to make it still
more dazzling. The sight drew from the old man
a cry of surprise and admiration, and his daughter felt prouder than a queen on seeing the joy
expressed in his face.

The first attempt had been too successful for
her to stop there. She worked with an ardor
which increased continually; for, according to the
fairy's promise, wherever her hands went, they
wrought marvels. She began by sweeping the
floor, upon which the rough stones turned to
beautiful squares of marble of different colors,
which joined together and formed a beautiful mo-
saic pavement. Next came the turn of the ceiling.
No sooner was it touched by the broom than the
black rafters became polished oak relieved with
threads of gold; the rough mortar was transform-

ed into brilliant stucco, and the spider's webs turned to charming landscapes. A magnificent paper, with satin figures, and a blue and satin border, soon covered the wall; the mantle-piece turned to beautiful Italian marble, and rosewood and velvet easy-chairs, sofas, and lounges took the place of the worn-out furniture.

Exhausted at last with fatigue and delight, Blanche threw herself on a luxurious velvet divan, which had been hitherto an old, broken, and rickety rush-bottomed chair, and clapped her hands with a fresh and joyous burst of laughter. Her father, who had silently followed her with his eyes from the beginning, seated himself beside her, and, taking her head in his trembling hands, kissed her forehead. A warm tear which fell on her cheek would have rewarded her for all this labor had not the labor itself lavished on her so rich a reward.

At this moment old Betty appeared to prepare the dinner. In her first astonishment she threw up her hands, opened her eyes and mouth, and stood still, unable to utter a word. "Oh!" she cried at length, "where did all these fine things come from, my dear good young lady?"

"I found them by doing your work, Betty, and I mean to continue. Let me cook the dinner; you may come back and wash the dishes."

Blanche set to work to rummage the cupboard, looking for the butter in one direction, and the meat in another, and tasting the little jars to distinguish the salt from the powdered sugar, for she knew the place of nothing. The apprenticeship lasted a full quarter of an hour, and after she had found every thing it was not a small task to light the fire. But she had no reason to regret her trouble when, after having made many trials, and more than once burned her fingers, she was finally ready to lay the cloth on a beautiful polished mahogany table, which had taken the place of the old rickety pine stand. The old man was at a loss to recognize the damask linen, cut-glass goblets, chased silver, and fine porcelain which covered the table in the place of the old service. His eyes rested with special pleasure on the slices of beautiful bread, as white as snow, with a crisp golden crust, which took the place of the heavy, indigestible paste, his habitual terror. I do not exactly remember what dish appeared for dinner —whether a haunch of venison, or a fat pullet stuffed with truffles—but, whatever it was, it seemed fit for a king to the two guests, who declared that they had never eaten its like.

They were still praising it when old Betty returned. She cleared the table with a respectful air, and, without joining in the conversation according to her usual custom, began to wash the dishes.

Suddenly Blanche ran to her with a cry of horror. The unfortunate old woman was undoing all her work. In her hands, which had not been gifted by the fairy, the fine porcelain had again become coarse earthen-ware, the spoons and forks were nothing but battered iron, what was left of the delicious bread was changed to a piece of a heavy loaf, and the so-much-boasted dish to a greasy stew.

"Thanks for your trouble, Betty. To-morrow morning I will send you to the village to do the errands; the rest I will take care of myself."

She heaved a faint sigh on plunging her beautiful white hands into the hot dish-water, but she did not shrink; all the comfort which she had procured for her father was well worth such a sacrifice.

Having repaired the evil by touching anew every piece of her beautiful service, she said to her father, "Now I am going to make your bed, that I may be sure that you will sleep well."

Half an hour after the happy old man took possession of a downy bed, furnished with soft blankets, large pillows, and fragrant linen, in which he slept soundly till morning.

On opening his eyes he saw his daughter employed in brushing his old clothes, and he was not a little surprised to find them quite new on rising.

I need not describe to you all the happiness that reigned in the house. Blanche went about singing, proud of her power, and wholly absorbed in the care of her treasures. Her father felt himself young again, and gazed at his brave child with an air of respectful gratitude that would have brought tears to your eyes.

Early in the morning the fairy appeared at the door, and made a sign to Blanche, who hastened to join her. They went together behind the house, where, pointing to the waste ground, "Now," said the fairy, "it is time to think of what is out of doors. The country is ready and willing to blossom like a rose, but you must aid it."

"What can I do?" asked Blanche. "I have never touched the earth."

"You must touch it, my child. It is the only way of making its acquaintance."

She gave her a little spade that she held in her hand, and a bag filled with packages of seeds, on which she blew three times, then disappeared.

This was also a very laborious day; but at sunset all was finished, and, with a joyful voice, the good girl called her father, who started with surprise at the sight of a miraculous garden, such as no gardener could have made. Every thing had put forth by enchantment. The trees were already fully grown, and covered with leaves and fruit, and the birds had even built their nests in them. The walls, entirely repaired, were hidden under trellises laden with apples, pears, peaches, and apricots, and a choice grape-vine covered the house with its green leaves and ripe clusters which seemed inviting the hand to gather them.

They wandered through the walks, bordered with great bunches of luscious strawberries, and the beautiful gardener named to her father all the flowers as she gathered the choicest to make him a huge bouquet. She finally led him to a turfy bank, shaded by a thick clump of walnut-trees, and there they silently witnessed the setting of the sun, which sank behind the mountains into a fiery sea. A linnet chirped above their heads, and in the distance they heard the shepherd's horn calling the sheep scattered over the pasture.

"Thank you, my beloved child," said the old man, clasping his daughter's hands, already a little freckled. He could say no more, but their eyes met, and they smiled as the angels must smile in Paradise.

The next morning came new labor and new triumph, somewhat dearly bought, it is true. The fairy again appeared, and offering the little workwoman a pair of stout shoes and a little scraper, like those used by the street-sweepers, she pointed to the horrible road in front of the house, then disappeared.

This time Blanche's heart revolted at the task. She saw, in her thoughts, her fine lady friends, and the proud gentlemen who had formerly fluttered round her, disdainfully passing in single file before the street-sweeper, and it seemed to her that it would be in the paper the next morning. There was no need of the fear of ridicule to frighten her, indeed; the vile mud of the street disgusted her quite enough without this. If the fairy had been there she would have doubtless found a thousand good reasons for giving her back her unlucky present. But what was she to do? The fairy was far off, and she could not risk displeasing her by disobedience after so many favors. She at last resigned herself to her fate, put on the stout shoes, and, carefully shutting the door that her father might not see her, bravely attacked the mud with her scraper.

Instantly, as if at the sound of a bell, the men and women came from all the houses, each with a shovel or a broom, and began to clean the road with all their might. At the end of an hour there was not a spot of mud to be seen as far as the eye could reach, and the road, dry, graveled, and smooth as a garden-walk, had become the pleasantest promenade that any one could desire.

A joyous cry brought Blanche's father to the threshold. Without giving him time to admire her work, she took him by the arm and led him into her beautiful new road. It was the first time that he had set his foot out of doors since he had come to the village. He had not before felt the courage to venture among all this mud, and it was to him a true voyage of discovery. The weather was magnificent. The little river that watered the meadow glittered in the sun like a silver ribbon; the birds were singing in the trees, and the fragrance of the new-mown hay was borne on the wind to the promenaders.

"We can still be happy here," said the father. "Thanks to thee, dear child," he added, in a voice full of emotion.

After walking a long distance, they were returning slowly, enjoying all around them at their ease, when their neighbor's child saw them coming, and ran to meet them.

"Oh, what a dirty child!" cried the old man. "I would not touch him with a pair of tongs."

Blanche gently drew the boy to her, passed her handkerchief over his face, and ran her fingers through his hair, and said, presenting him to her father,

"You did not look at him well, papa. See how pretty he is!"

Indeed, she had cleansed him in the twinkling of an eye as had never been done before, and nothing could have been imagined more beautiful than the little urchin, with his rosy cheeks, his large blue eyes at once shy and saucy, his golden curls finer and softer than silk, and his little laughing mouth. God has made friendship easy between old men and children, because he wishes them to keep each other company. Attracted by the sight of so much loveliness, the old man involuntarily leaned forward and opened his arms, into which the child threw himself, smiling.

The friendship was formed, and they carried their little companion to his own door, where his father received him with a coarse, insolent laugh.

"How can such a brute have so beautiful a

child ?" murmured the nobleman, seating himself on the turfy bank in his garden.

"Let me introduce him to you, papa," said Blanche. And, walking straight to the countryman, who looked at her with an air of astonishment, she took him by the hand, and said, graciously, "Will you not be kind enough, sir, to take your child to my father?"

What was the surprise of the proud old man to see the brute of the moment before transformed into a sensible and polite man, whose manners were nobler in their simplicity than that of many vulgar rich men whom he had seen strutting about their drawing-rooms. His eye beamed with intelligence, his stupid laugh had given place to a thoughtful and serious expresssion, and, drawing himself up to his full length, he listened with flattering attention to what was said to him. The simple contact with the enchanted hand had changed him from head to foot.

They talked for a long time, the countryman listening with interest to what was told him of the city, and telling them many things about the country which were new to them. The child at first had clung to Blanche's dress, and, kept in check by the presence of her father, who did not play with him, finally fell asleep on his lap. When their neighbor took his leave with his sleeping child in his arms, it was as a friend, and the poor exiles were no longer alone in the world.

You will think, perhaps, that miracles enough had been wrought, and that the fairy ought to have been satisfied with what she had done for her pupil. But this did not appear to her sufficient. She appeared again, this time with a great market-basket, and, putting it into Blanche's hand,

"This is my last gift," said she, "and it will not disgrace the others. Go and make your own purchases, and silver will become gold in your hands."

She obeyed. Every morning she was seen setting out for market with her great basket on her arm, and, as silver became gold in her hands, the household in future lacked for nothing. The tradesmen, who loved her for her pleasant manners and her honest dealing, always put aside for her the best that they had in their shops. Every one honored her, for she had been greatly respected in the village since she had been seen so courageous in work and so devoted to her father, and the inventor of the jest about Jack and his daughter knew not where to hide his head.

One day the king's son chanced to pass that way as Blanche was returning home with her great basket on her arm. He remembered having formerly danced with her at the court balls, and I even believe that at that time he had not been wholly indifferent to her; but he had been ignorant of her father's ruin, for so many events take place about kings that some escape them. Surprised at meeting his beautiful partner in such a place, he made inquiries about her of the people of the place, who could not find enough to say in her praise. They told him how she had saved her father from the horrors of poverty, and related to them all the marvels that had sprung up at her touch. He went away musing, and dreamed all night of a little white hand that wrought miracles.

Winter came, and the good old man became weaker every day. The cold became severe, and as his dress was thin, Blanche was obliged to go to town to buy him warmer clothing. It was a long journey, and if she could, she would have gladly sent some one in her place, for she disliked to leave her father for a whole day in his state of health. But her hand alone had the privilege of changing silver to gold, and when any one is poor he is often obliged to do things the very idea of which would be shocking to the rich.

She set out, therefore, early one morning, after urging their neighbor's wife to take good care of her father, and showing her where to find every thing that he might need. She walked fast all day through the streets of the city, buying all that she could think of to make him comfortable.

It was night before she returned, worn out with her journey; but, without stopping to put down the great bundle that she carried, she ran to her father, whom she saw stretched on the bed. The neighbor's wife was standing by his side, trying to make him swallow some medicine, evidently ordered by the doctor, for the prescription was still on the table; but he seemed not to see her, and fixed his haggard eyes on the wall. Blanche looked that way, when what was her terror to see Death standing by the bed, grasping the old man by the throat, and saying, with a cruel laugh,

"Make haste; I am in a hurry. Come with me into the ground."

The poor child felt her heart wrung at this horrible sight, but she took care not to give way when she was so much needed. Dropping her bundle, she took the medicine from the neighbor, and put it with one hand to her father's lips, while with the other she smoothed the pillows. He knew her, and drank it with a smile. When she raised her eyes, the terrible spectre had given place to a beautiful woman clothed in white, whose pale and emanciated face bore an expression of enchanting sweetness. One of her hands was laid on the old man's shoulder, and with the other she pointed to the sky, while her full blue eye rested on him with an inviting glance.

"Where do you wish to carry me?" he asked, with lingering fear.

"You will know directly. Do not tremble; it will not be painful."

He appeared quieted, and already his face lighted up with solemn joy, when his eye fell on Blanche, who was weeping in silence, and his features clouded with sorrow at the thought that she would be left alone. But at that moment the good fairy stood at his pillow, and, bending over, whispered in his ear, "I will take care of her."

He smiled, and fell asleep with a smile on his lips and his hand in that of his daughter.

When the neighbors came to carry him to the grave, his courageous daughter accompanied him to the end, and, the ceremonies ended, she set to work to beautify his new abode. In a little time his tomb was covered with flowers and verdure; branches of ivy crept around it, and dwarf roses, pansies, violets, and myrtle covered the turf between two little firs which raised their green feathery heads at each end of the grave. It was the last service that her hands could render to her beloved father, and, this done, she slowly retraced her steps, dreading to return.

On the threshold of the house she found the queen awaiting her, with her maids of honor. "I have heard of you," said her majesty, kissing her on the forehead, "and I have come to take you to my palace. I shall esteem myself happy to be the mother of a daughter like you."

The queen seated her in her golden carriage by her side, and they set out, followed by the villagers, who loaded Blanche with praise and blessings.

She afterward married the king's son, and had a magnificent court, splendid gardens, and apartments a thousand times more brilliant than those of her first prosperity. But in the midst of all this prosperity she sometimes seemed dreary, and when her maids sought to know the reason,

"I was thinking of the time when I was Jack's daughter," said she. "I shall never be so happy again."

THE TWO FRIENDS.

THERE were once two friends, a blonde and a brunette, Gabrielle and Ernestine, who had been brought up together, and who loved each other dearly, but not in the same way. Ernestine was all fire, so violent in her affection that she almost smothered her friend in her embraces; but she was very imperious, and would not endure contradiction, but flew into a passion at the least resistance, and swept away every thing before her. Gabrielle, who was as gentle as a lamb, let her do as she pleased, bore her caresses and her anger, and never tired of yielding to her, for she loved her so much that she could not live without her.

One day, however, when the impetuous Ernestine flew into a passion with a little girl in the neighborhood, and threatened to strike her, because she had not stepped aside soon enough to let her pass, Gabrielle took up the defense of the oppressed child, who was weak and timid, and who had already began to cry, whereupon she at once received orders never to speak to the little unfortunate. As this appeared to her unjust and wicked, she declared that she would not obey.

Nothing more was needed to bring about a quarrel. After a terrible scene of rage on one side, and tears on the other, the passionate Ernestine solemnly declared that all was over, and that she never wished to see Gabrielle again in all her life. She then ran to her mother complaining bitterly of her ungrateful friend, and insisting on being taken to the play that evening to drive away her sorrow. Wherever she went, she gave vent to new complaints, and bursts of grief so heart-rending that her friends thought of nothing but inventing amusements to divert her, so that her trouble furnished the occasion of a continual round of festivities.

The poor forsaken Gabrielle returned home without saying a word, and quietly went about her usual occupations, without speaking of her sorrow, smiling whenever it would make others happy, and never mentioning her lost friend. But she grew paler day by day; her appetite failed, and her strength declined; and, in the end, her parents called in the doctor, who declared that she was ill, and ordered her to take to her bed. There, at liberty to abandon herself to her grief, she soon grew worse. She speedily became so weak that her life was despaired of, and, scarcely able to speak, she at last murmured her friend's name, and asked that she might be brought to her.

Her weeping parents hastened in search of Ernestine, whom they found in the midst of a children's party, which had been made expressly to console her grief.

Ernestine at first refused to go. "I am too sensitive," said she. "In spite of the suffering she has caused me, I have loved her so dearly that I can not endure to see her ill in bed. Tell her that I forgive her, and that I will go to see her as soon as she is well." But Gabrielle's parents would not excuse her, and she finally set out in her gauze dress.

At the sight of little Gabrielle's pale, wan face, as white as wax and almost as transparent, her heart suddenly melted, and she burst into tears. Throwing herself on the bed, she clasped the sick girl convulsively in her arms. She hurt her, but the poor child did not seem to perceive it. Her face lighted up, and the roses began to return to her cheeks.

"Oh! my dear Gabrielle, my dear friend, speak; what is it that ails you?" cried Ernestine.

"I believe that it is partly my sorrow on your account," answered Gabrielle, gently. "But you are here now, and I shall soon be well again." And from that moment she began to recover.

THE GREAT SCHOLAR.

THERE was once a little boy by the name of Leon, who was always at the head of his class. He gained all the prizes—the grammar prize, the arithmetic prize, the history prize, the geography prize—and went home on examination-day with a great pile of books under his arm, and so many wreaths on his head that you could hardly see him. The people in the streets turned to look at him as he passed, and the next day, at market, the nurse talked with great pride about her young master, who was already a great scholar. All this puffed up the heart of the poor little boy, and gave him a great opinion of himself.

A little girl by the name of Rose, who lived in the neighborhood, often came to play with him. She did not learn as easily as he, but she was a darling little child, gentle and loving to every body, and obedient to her parents; and who, every night before going to sleep, always prayed to God with all her heart to make her wise and good. The great scholar soon began to look down on her. One day he took it into his head that an ignorant little girl like her must be very much beneath him, and that it would be well to find out what she knew before continuing to honor her with his company; and, the dear child having come to show him a beautiful picture-book which her godmother had given her, he received her with a cold and haughty air which was quite new to poor Rose.

"I shall be glad to look at the pictures," said he, "but first I want to know whether you can change a vulgar fraction to a decimal?"

Rose burst out laughing. "Oh, I haven't been so far as that," said she. "I am just going to begin division."

"You needn't laugh; I am in earnest. At least you can tell me the difference between a relative leading proposition and an absolute leading proposition?"

"We were told the other day in the class, but I have forgotten."

"Very well. It is probably of no use to ask you in what year Rome was founded?"

"What a ridiculous question! You know very well that I have only just begun the history of Egypt."

"Worse and worse. I am almost sure that you can not tell me the names of the states in the Valley of the Mississippi?"

She remained mute; her geographical knowledge did not yet extend to the Valley of the Mississippi.

"Oh dear," said she, at length, "what is the matter with you to-day? We are not in school; leave all these things alone, and come and see my picture-book; it is full of pretty stories."

"Dear Rose," answered Leon, with a condescending air, "in the first place, I don't care for stories any longer. In the next place, you must own that I know a great deal more than you do. It is not proper that we should be seen any more together."

Poor little Rose could find no other answer

than a fit of crying, for she loved Leon dearly, and it seemed very hard to lose him on account of the Valley of the Mississippi and the relative proposition. As she was looking at him with an imploring eye, unable to make up her mind to go without him, her godmother suddenly entered.

This was a respectable old lady, of great merit, although she was but little known, which will not surprise you when I tell you her name; she was called the fairy Modesty. She was not very partial to those distributions of prizes, from which children return home with laurel-wreaths on their heads, proud and triumphant like victorious generals. Nevertheless she said nothing, for, though modesty is an admirable thing in itself, it is not a sufficient weapon in the battle of life; and it is also necessary to inspire children with ardor and emulation if we would make men of them. She therefore let them wear their laurels, knowing well that modesty would some day come of itself to the great; while as to the others, it would be cruelty, she thought, to deprive them of the little vainglory which would serve as their consolation.

The vexation of her dear goddaughter, however, had touched her, and she came to punish the proud boy who was the cause of her tears.

"So you know nothing, my dear little Rose,"

said she. "Well, can you tell me what we must do to lead a good life?"

"Oh, godmamma, that is not hard. We must obey God, and be kind, like Him, to every one."

"That is knowing something; but I can understand that it is not enough to make you a fit companion for so learned a boy as Leon. Come with me, sir," she added, turning to Leon; "you know too much, it is true, to associate with little girls. What suits you now is the society of scholars and authors."

Saying this, she took him by the hand, and he suddenly found himself transported to one of the rooms of a great observatory, where a man of imposing appearance was seated at a long table before a heap of papers covered with figures. This man was truly a great scholar. He had taken the measure of the globe—a work far more difficult than the Rule of Three. He had followed the march of the light, which travels seventy-two thousand leagues in a second, and had calculated how many years it would take us to reach the nearest star. With pen in hand, he weighed the sun and moon as in a balance, and by calculation found the route of the heavenly bodies through the boundless space which surrounds us.

The fairy Modesty bowed to him. He smiled in a friendly manner, and greeted her like an old acquaintance.

"Good-morning, master," said she. "Here is a scholar who desires to have some conversation with you."

The great man knew of no more lively pleasure than that of imparting his knowledge to all who desired it. He gave his hand to the little boy.

"I congratulate you," said he. "A scholar at your age! it is really wonderful. Will you help me find a comet that we have been expecting for the last month? I am just trying to discover what can have stopped it on its way. We will look for it together."

To look for comets was rather beyond Leon, who had gone no farther than the Rule of Interest. He blushed and declined the proposal.

"Well, we will talk of optics, acoustics, or hydrostatics, as you please."

The poor humbled child knew not where to hide his head.

"You know logarithms, at least?"

He replied, trying to restrain his tears, that he did not understand these stupid things, but that he could change a vulgar fraction to a decimal.

The learned man looked at the fairy with an air of surprise, and was about to ask her what kind of scholar she had brought him; but she did not leave him time to speak.

"Master," said she, "I know a little girl who

says that to lead a good life we must obey God, and be kind, like Him, to every one. Do you know any more about it than she does?"

"God forbid that I should think so! The dear child has said all there is to say on the subject."

"Let us go," said the fairy to her companion.

They instantly entered a large house inhabited by a great historian. Nothing was to be seen any where, from the cellar to the attic, but books ranged in order on shelves nailed to the wall in all possible places. There were some so large that a man could hardly lift them. There were others so small that they could be carried in the vest pocket. There were specimens of every style of covers made since the invention of bookbinding—yellow, red, black, white, and all colors—of parchment, calf, carved wood, embossed leather, and gilt morocco with silver clasps. There were even some of those old books of the time of the Romans, written on strips of bark, with each end wound on wooden rollers, which the reader turned in opposite directions as he advanced. Those who could read these books could boast of being learned.

They went first into a large room devoted to the history of the Egyptians, Phœnicians, Babylonians, and Persians; and to read all the books there, their owner had been obliged to learn Hebrew, Arabic, ancient and modern Persian, and many more languages, the names of which I have forgotten. He knew, of course, how to decipher the hieroglyphics on the Egyptian obelisks; but all this did not satisfy him; he could not forgive himself for not having learned Chinese. Next came the room of Greek History, and naturally the historian understood Greek; then the room of Roman History, and I need not tell you that he understood Latin — not only the Latin that is learned at college, but also the old Latin of the earliest days of Rome, which the best college graduate does not understand a bit better than if he had never opened a Latin dictionary in all his life. They saw, besides, a long row of other rooms, devoted each to the history of a nation, and on the next floor above there were as many more; but they went no farther. The historian was in the Roman-History room, absorbed in a huge German book which any one else might have found very tiresome, but which must have been very interesting to him, since he did not perceive their presence till they were close upon him.

Confounded at the sight of so many books, poor Leon had begged the fairy not to introduce him as a scholar—him who had read nothing but the little school history.

When the great historian raised his head and

saw the fairy Modesty, he eagerly threw down his book, and stretched out his hand as if to an old friend.

"Welcome!" he exclaimed; "I know only too well how much I need you."

"Master," said she, "here is a little boy who is not yet a scholar, but he knows nevertheless in what year Rome was founded."

The historian smiled gently. "Are you quite sure of the year, my little friend?"

"Oh yes, very sure; I recited the whole page yesterday without making a single mistake."

"Well, you are more learned than I, for I am not wholly sure of it. There are some men even who, by dint of studying, have come to the conclusion that Romulus never existed; but I think that they go too far."

Leon looked amazed. The historian stretched his hand toward the mountain of books that rose from the floor to the ceiling. "If you knew only one quarter of the errors and falsehoods which are there, my dear child," said he, "you would be less astonished at my words. Those who know nothing are the only ones that have no doubts."

"Master," said the fairy, "I know a little girl who says that to lead a good life we must obey God, and be kind, like Him, to every one. Do you doubt what she says?"

"God forbid! No one can doubt the dear child's words."

The young scholar began to find himself in an awkward position. "I see, my dear child," said the malicious fairy, "that these men are too much for you. I will take you to the greatest writer of the age; she will terrify you less, and you can talk about grammar with her."

The greatest writer of the age was a woman. This will perhaps appear incredible, especially as men do not willingly acknowledge that such a thing can be; this time, however, they were obliged to admit it.

She received the fairy Modesty with great cordiality in a room which looked like any other parlor, and the little boy felt quite at his ease on seeing himself in the presence of a very simply-dressed lady, who had nothing remarkable about her but her large and brilliant black eyes. His first two discomfitures, however, had rendered him timid, and he dared not speak first.

"Madam," said the fairy, "here is a child who knows grammar thoroughly. He would be glad to talk to you about the rules of our language."

The lady, who was full of indulgence to children, laughed. "I shall not appear to very good advantage in such a conversation," answered she. "I write what comes to my mind, and do not trouble myself much about rules. Yet, if it will give you pleasure, my little fellow, I have no objection. Of what would you like to talk?"

"I can explain the difference between an absolute leading proposition and a relative leading proposition," said he.

She burst into a hearty fit of laughter. "When I was a child," said she, "we did not trouble ourselves about all these rhetorical rules. I do not know exactly how to define them, and I can very well dispense with knowing."

The fairy interfered to put an end to the embarrassment of the child, who knew not which way to look. "I know a little girl, madam," said she, "who says that to lead a good life we must obey God, and be kind, like Him, to every one. Do you think that we can dispense with what she says we ought to do?"

"Unfortunately, there are too many who do so, but, in one way or another, they are always punished for it. The dear child! I would give her a good hearty kiss if she were here. What she says is necessary for all mankind."

"Thus far we have been unfortunate," said the fairy to the discomfited grammarian, "but we will not be discouraged yet. We must go through all your accomplishments."

He suddenly felt himself swept away by a

whirlwind. When he recovered his senses he was in a large hall, of a magnificent style of architecture, with strange maps suspended on the walls on all sides. He recognized the general outlines of the continents, but he did not find a single one of the geographical divisions to which his eye was accustomed.

"Where are we?" said he to the fairy.

"In the midst of Africa, my dear child, at present the most civilized country of the globe, and this is one of the school-rooms of the country. Don't be astonished; I have carried you two thousand years in advance of the epoch in which you were living a little while ago."

At the same instant the doors opened, and the scholars entered in a body, the boys on one side, and the girls on the other. They were dark and fair, rosy and pale, large and small, quiet and noisy, just as now; but all had a white skin.

"I thought that the people in Africa were black," said Leon.

"It is a long time now since the white race took possession of all the earth, and what you have read in your geographies no longer has any meaning."

The schoolmaster entered in turn. He was a man of tall stature, richly dressed, and wearing two decorations on his breast; for the office of schoolmaster was one of the most honorable in the country, and the most eminent men applied in crowds whenever a post was vacant. The candidates were formed into a class, and the children made their choice from among them.

The recitation commenced, and Leon, who had not expected to understand a word, was quite surprised to hear his own language. This did not help him much, it is true. All the names were changed, and great cities, celebrated rivers, and flourishing nations were mentioned of which he had never heard.

The fairy, who saw his anxiety, hastened to speak. " Master," said she, " do you not teach the children the names of the states in the Valley of the Mississippi?"

The teacher, who was a man of merit, made a low bow to the fairy Modesty, as is the custom with men of merit in all ages.

" I have seen the Mississippi mentioned in a very old geography," said he, " but one which is full of errors, and which betrays the ignorance of the times, since absolutely nothing is found in it concerning our great country. But the states of which you speak long since ceased to exist. All that country was sunk at the time of the great earthquake in the year 2500, and the fishes are now swimming above the capitals of the ancient states."

"And you, my child," said the fairy, addressing a little girl who was paying close attention to the lesson, "can you tell me what we must do to lead a good life?"

"We must obey God," answered the child, "and be kind, like Him, to every one."

She had scarcely done speaking when Leon found himself again in his room with the fairy, in the presence of Rose, who still looked at him with an imploring glance.

"Do you not think now," said the fairy, "that her knowledge is worth as much as yours? You have been able yourself to measure the value of what you know, and those men before whom you were as nothing have bowed respectfully before her knowledge. No one knows more than she on this subject, no one doubts it, no one can dispense with it, and it will not have changed one iota two thousand years from now."

"Then there is no need of taking so much trouble at school," returned Leon, somewhat ill-naturedly, "since this is all the value to be set on what I learn there."

"Ah!" said the fairy, laughing, "I was sure that you would come to that conclusion. No, my child, you must not reason in this way. These men, whose learning awes you, knew no more than you when they were of your age. If they had not studied then as you are doing, they would know nothing now; and it is only by continuing to learn well that you will some day become as learned as they. That lady, who did not understand the words which you had learned, had learned others which expressed the same thing perhaps even better. And that the earth will change after you are gone is no reason that you should not study it. All your friends will change, and so will you; is that any reason why you should not live now as comrades? I only wished to show you that you were wrong in being so proud of your poor little knowledge, and, above all, in setting it above the knowledge of goodness of heart—the only kind that is certain, that is necessary, that can not be dispensed with, and that will never change. Now kiss my goddaughter, and go to see the pictures; you have well earned the pleasure."

Leon kissed Rose, who clasped him tenderly in her arms. He went to see the pictures, with which he was delighted, and read the stories, which taught him many things that he did not know. And afterward, when his nurse called him a great scholar in his presence, he said to himself that there was but one kind of learning, the same for great and small—*to obey God, and to be kind, like Him, to every one.*